LOVE THE SINNER

LOVE THE SINNER

by Mo Moshaty

To Algernon, thanks for the imagination. To Muddy, thanks for the soundtrack. To Clive, thanks for the heart.

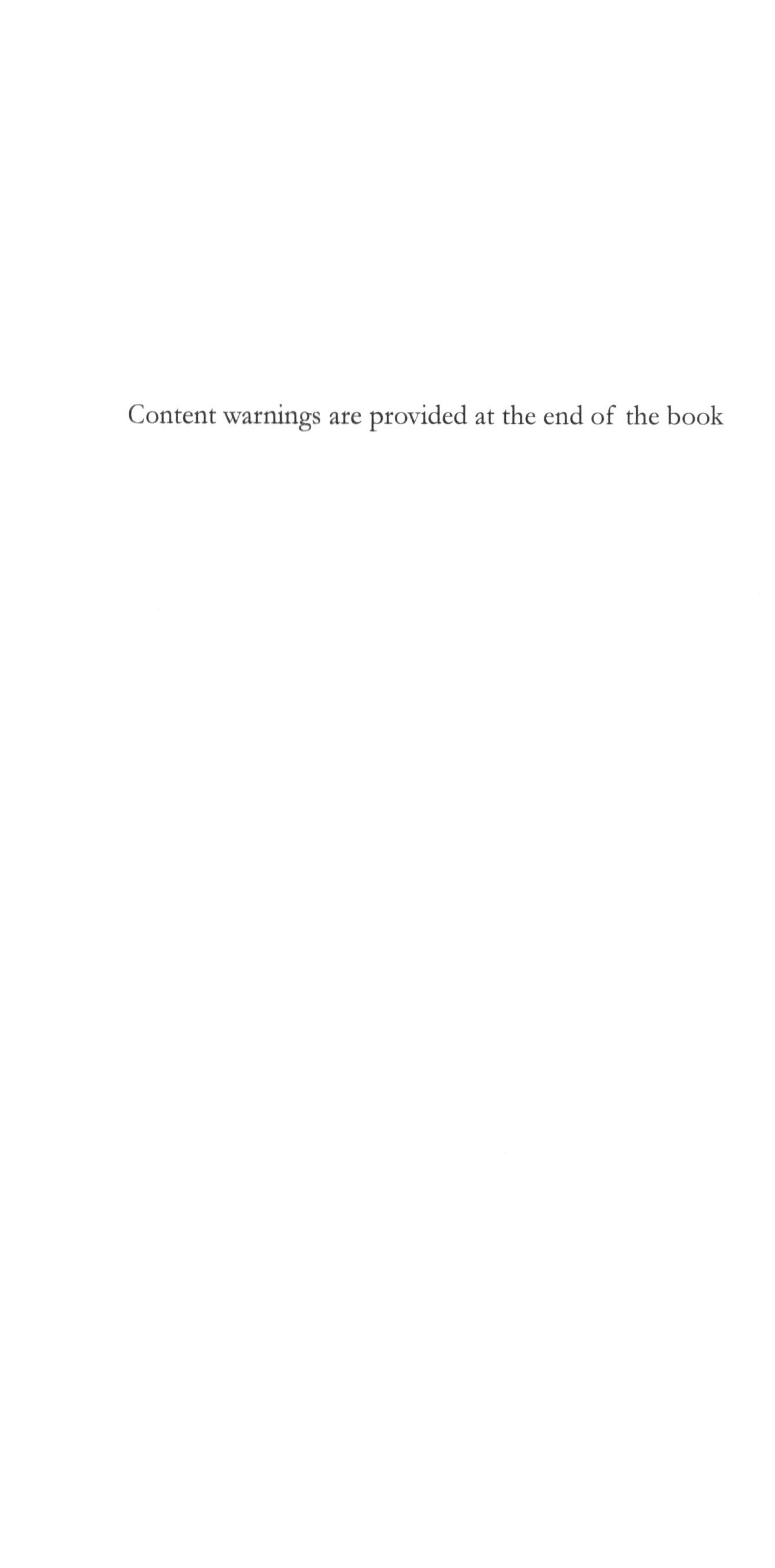

Content warnings are provided at the end of the book

CONTENTS

Suicide

What is the mark of man, really? Strength, agility, resiliency?

Well, then. I am not a man, more of a shell rather. A lot of us are. I put on a helmet and boots and was asked to do the unthinkable when I can't even make my bed most days. And it's everything, most days. Simple, easy most days. Achingly unbearable, the volume of the shouting in my head and the blood in my eyes. Always the blood in my eyes. Those poor boys.

It's always a senseless fight, and for some reason, it's always a boy they ask to fight it … most days.

—Private First-Class Greg Burns, A Journal, 1947

A BATTLE BETWEEN BOYS

I'd been running with MacArthur in tow for fifty yards along the beach before I'd realized it was just a chest and an arm. Pulling like hell, the heft of him couldn't have mattered less. He was almost cloud-like, weightless, like dragging along boardwalk cotton candy. As I stopped, taking shield from a burnt-out Jeep, all the mangled uselessness of him seemed like an anvil in my arms. I noticed his father's watch, a non-working relic left over from WWI, almost glistening in the dust-ridden atmosphere. I laid the carcass down and ran as fast as I could in the midst of men on fire and dirt flying, weaving through a hundred mutilated MacArthur's still stinking of sea water and screaming until my lungs heaved.

"Mr. Burns! Mr. Burns?" Doris Garson from 14B stood nervously above me.

"Doris?" The number of Doris's began to shrink into one, and suddenly my body felt quite wet. "Doris? Doris, I'm alright." I stood, bearing most of my weight along the elevator wall.

Oh God. Not again.

"You have that dream again?" She backed away slowly with a tight smile. Too kind to scold me, and too petrified to escape.

"I suppose I have. I'm so sorry to frighten you so." I'd squeezed my coat at the cuffs, creating wet stains, and I had barricaded myself behind my luggage. I kicked it to either side of me gently.

"Such a pity, those dreams." She clung lightly to the opposite wall. "A trip?" She glanced at the weather-worn suitcase and kit bag and stared at me, almost begging for a trip to be true. She gripped her purse handle tighter.

"Yes, up north for a bit. Some R&R." I attempted a smile that mistakenly bared teeth.

The bell rang for the ground floor and the doors parted. "Have a lovely trip!" Doris Garson parted the elevator without looking back and scuttled out of the building.

My fifth such encounter with her. My fifth witness to an unending dream and the fact that I was slowly going completely mad.

"Getting back to nature, they call it," I said and puffed out my chest comically. "You know, like men of old. None of this trolley car and wingtip business."

"Since when have you ever been like that, Greg? You've caught more of a fuss about hair out of place than the whole missed deadline of the Crossing account." Kent Willingham mime-punched me in the stomach.

"Alright, enough!" I exclaimed.

I gestured to my baggage at the side of my desk. A shoddy suitcase full of marked-down meat. A kit bag, with three changes of clothes, two pairs of boots, soups, bread, coffee, and beans. PFC Burns was shipping off again.

"That there, gentlemen, is the start of new things. R&R and not a moment too soon. I've been looking for a little since O'Malley, and I think this ought to do it," I said.

"That true?" Tommy Wilson asked. "That he just never came back? Just went in the woods and never came back? You ain't thinkin' he—"

"Boys, boys, this is quite different than Tommy O'Malley hitting the drink in a half-cocked headspace somewhere on his grandfather's camp. I'm alright, just need some peace. Holidays are coming and we've a ton of print ads to look at for Wanamaker's."

And with that, everyone shuffled back to their desks in a slow buzz, like worker bees getting back to the tedious business. I was grateful for my heavy coat with the canvas cuffs. Silly to have pulled it out so early in October, but I was glad for it. When I emerged from Kastor and Sons, the snow was pounding at a faster pace than I would've liked, but it was beautiful. A cascade of crystalline fireflies in the afternoon. Some twinkling, others dashing away at the first contact. I had the urge to stick my tongue out and let it gently transport me back to gliding on the ice in the park, Mother looking on. But I decided against it, the snow took a sideways turn and people hurried across the streets. I hopped into the car side-saddle and shook what I could off my shoes before the snow snuck in the door.

I should have left earlier. The mill road was always clear up this way, I'd heard, and I was forty miles outside the city by now. It was as clear as lentil soup, but the car was staying steady yet slow, so I stopped complaining. Another hour of white-knuckled jitters and I'd be there. A little respite, some R&R, I told them. A wicked lie. A winter storm was chasing me. I had to reach the place and start a fire before the worst of it came. I needed this time away to think— or not think, I couldn't decide.

I sang all the records I knew to myself. One made me quite sad, and I stopped, I didn't remember the name. Something my mother used to love, about bugles, I think.

I was just trailing off when I came to it. The bright red ribbons hanging from the tall evergreen at the edge of the property. Just like he'd said. They swayed sharply in the winter wind like blood-red gashes against a steely wall of snow.

I stared at the cabin, much smaller than had been described, and more desolate. But it looked quiet enough and a fire could change the frigidity of it. I set off down the small hill, slipping a bit. I'd dropped a can of soup but decided to leave it. It'd be there tomorrow. I had read that the snow would be getting worse, and I had my heart set on battening down and watching my coffee steam over views of evergreens and streams.

The cabin exhaled staleness and must. I set my things down at the entrance, bewildered by the design of the place. Each area cordoned to its own corner of the cabin like directional stewards facing each other, with a helm of two chairs across from the tall hearth. Stacked high to the ceiling was firewood in perfect pie slices, as promised. I hurried over, grabbed four pieces, and tossed them in. I ruffled through my kit bag for the can of gas and my overcoat's inner breast pocket for the matches. A crackling fire and a smoke would do me fine.

The fire started easily. A little gas does the trick every time. Doesn't smell too good but it beat out the stale scent of dread I felt when I walked in. Something had happened here. Maybe a million tragic things. Maybe nothing. Maybe just one undiscovered death right in that bed in the corner. Or maybe I was falling again. I'd been doing that lately. For about a year now. Falling, falling, falling. Sometimes, simple things like not remembering where I left something, sometimes shouting and screaming at people and seeing things no one else can see, troubling and horrifying poor old-timers like Doris. It might happen like that, they said, the doctors who looked at us on the train back from the front line. It was happening to Tommy too.

Rest. Rest and peace were all we were after.

But tonight, the falling was faster than it had been, and I had been hoping that this cabin, this house of leniency, would throw me a line.

I don't know how long the kettle had been boiling, or when I'd even set it to heat. It howled into view like a stereophonic headlight on a dark road. In this cabin with its notch-clad walls and exposed plaster and antlers of all sizes and shapes, a doe head looked quizzically at me. It made me laugh nervously. It was watching me. Something was watching me.

My mind was in shards, all pointing in different directions. I'd never let them see. My house was well-kept, but my inside was crumbling. Glowing and bent, out of focus like a child's cheap kaleidoscope.

Tommy O'Malley and I talked deeply. On the battlefield front line, on the train home. We'd ignored each other for a while. Both running from the things we'd seen. Both trying to make sense of seeing upright men become half their size without half their bodies and twice their blood and make headway and keep making headway and duck this way and that and fall in line and goddamn it, shoot them and just come home already. The coming home was harder than shooting a man dead. Ain't it crazy? Murdering. Easy. And that's why I sit out here now under this guise of reprieve. For Tommy.

We'd reconnected about six months ago. I'd taken a marketing job at Kastor and Sons. Writing copy for the *New York Daily*, mostly shopping ads but the pay was right, and I got a few suit coats in the closet now and it's all fine, exceptionally fine. Tommy had developed a slight tic that made his upper lip twitch if he sat still long enough. We needed an illustrator for some quick ads and Tommy fit the bill, and the team, perfectly. It was a dream being alongside him again, and the gang loved him. One week, a shipping trolley dropped a large palette of typewriters in the street. The noise sent Tommy under the desk, wheezing, and hacking and screaming. He'd come to work silently for the next few days, then had stopped completely.

He'd written to me before he disappeared that he was going to spend his days on his grandfather's plot of land, in the Adirondacks near a river rich with bass. It was almost lyrical how he painted the scene. Language rich, agile, and colorful, like the words of a man who's figured out the meaning of life, the end of it all, and with confidence and knowledge of what lies beyond. He was free. Signed Thomas D. O'Malley Private First Class.

I rolled out a hard metal object enclosed in the letter, it was wound with paper and string. One bullet. It read:

One for me, and one for you.

He saw me going through it too, he watched me panic in the men's room and throw papers anxiously in my apartment and sleep under the bed, waiting, waiting, waiting for those soldiers to come. He was inviting me to be free. This cabin was weather-worn and grey, no water too near, no lush property, no apple trees, no woodland musings, and creatures dancing about, like he'd said. And I'm sure he knew that. I know that now. His eyes showed him something different these days. And not another letter since July. It was obvious he hadn't been here long, if at all. The hearth was heavily cobwebbed. A layer of settled dust on everything. Not a stitch of food in the ice box. Where had he gone? Had he even come at all? Where was he leading me? Was this all a trap? The questions were burning my lips so strongly I hadn't realized I'd been shouting.

As I glanced out the only window of the cabin, I saw Tommy. Twenty paces away, staring in. His eyes wide and glowing like a lamp.

I clumsily stepped into my unlaced boots and ran out the door. He leapt away, his eyes lighting a path ahead of him. He laughed hardily, boyishly high-pitched.

"Come on!" Tommy shouted. "Come on! Hurry! Yahoo!"

My breath was ragged. I had forgotten my coat and my ankles were wet and freezing. I stopped to lace my boot and looked up to follow, but he was gone. His lights extinguished. He'd left me. Or I'd been too slow. I stood, damp and freezing, in an unfamiliar wood, my eyes searched in the darkness. A small amber glow behind me gave me pause. The cabin. I hadn't gone far.

I followed my footsteps back, one set only. I couldn't remember if Tommy ever touched the ground as he bounded. The firelight got stronger, and my bones warmed at the thought of sitting almost upon it when I came back in. But I stopped short, almost tumbling. Facing the fire with mirrored eyes sat Tommy, on one of the two chairs set in the entrance. His head turned towards me. He smiled and returned to watching the fire.

I stood outside for several minutes. Letting the pellets of snow sting my skin like a million hornets. Finally, I walked through and watched the way the fire made his silhouette dance.

"Hey Greg. Come in. You'll catch your death," Tommy said.

"Alright," I said.

"Sit, here with me. You've built a nice fire here, strong. Gas?"

"Yes," I murmured. I couldn't bring myself to speak in full voice, not yet. I sat cautiously, gripping the arms of the chair to slow my body down. This specter with emblazoned eyes was no more the man I knew than the can of gas that sat on the table. I was falling, no doubt. And I would have to prove that not only was I not falling, that I was completely upright.

"What happened to you?" I asked, hurriedly. Sometimes the body wants to ask things the mind knows it shouldn't, but if it stays inside any longer it can cause a combustion of fear and sinister ideas. Worry, in all its forms.

"I let go," he said. A slight smile on his lips. His eyes flickered and he finally looked in my direction. "I let go and stopped falling. I was going to keep falling. Falling and failing at trying to keep it together. Murder on the soul, really. To pretend you're alright, all the time. Makes you tired. And sick. Sick and tired, sick, and tired." He laughed, maniacally, then stopped.

"Is that why you're here, Greg?" He leaned his elbow on his knee and turned his body towards me. "To let go?"

"No. Rest. Rest is what I wanted." I tried more heft in my voice.

"Bah!" he shouted. "You could've rested at home. Or in a hotel for a week. Do you feel rested?"

"No." I looked at the rest of his face, his body. All the same Tommy. "Your eyes. What happened to your eyes?"

"My eyes?" Tommy asked. "I don't know. What's wrong with them?"

"They're glowing," I said.

He laughed again. "Oh yes. I'd forgotten. They just started doing that when I woke up that day."

"What day?" I asked.

"The day after I shot myself." Tommy's luminous gaze traveled around the room.

I stood quickly, knocking the gas onto the floor. I swept it up and screwed the top back on. My back was to him, and I could feel his eyes burn into me.

"Greg? You alright?" Tommy said calmly.

"No, I'm not alright, dammit! Offed yourself, eh? Figures." I was bellowing at Tommy as he stayed seated.

"Figures, how?" he asked. His voice was gentle, even-tempered, which sent me raging.

"Figures you'd leave me all alone! No one to talk to, to explain falling to. No one to stop it when it got bad."

"I couldn't save you, Greg. I could only save me. And even that was tiring. I was so tired when I came here." Tommy drew his attention back to the fire. "I remember lighting fires here with my grandfather. The last late summer fire when the wind comes in through the cracks and you know the leaves will start turning soon. And everything is new and reborn, like spring but grander somehow. More beautiful. The promise of turkey coming, of presents and snow. Promise. I was looking for promise here. Hope. I didn't find it. I was falling and running at the same time and my mind couldn't keep up anymore. And I was okay with that. To stop running. To stay still." Tommy turned his head back to me.

My mouth searched for a rebuttal, unfound.

I wanted to be angry. I wanted to tell him how much I loved him and how much I wanted him to stay and help each other stop falling and find a way to live again. Maybe he would move off and marry and I would do the same. And we would regale our children of the war one day, how brave we'd been to survive such a thing. Maybe we would meet as old men and remember, just for a while, then put it away to remember better things. Things we'd have done together.

"What did you bring here, Greg? Your kit bag looks full," Tommy said.

"Books mostly. A few changes of clothes and dungarees. Thick socks and a large sweater or two, a blanket."

"Show me," he said. "Empty out your kit bag, Greg."

"I'm sorry?" I asked.

I felt a lump in my throat and the bile behind it. I opened it slowly. Two pairs of socks. A blanket, dungarees rolled tightly, one blue sweater and one yellow, three undershirts and three pairs of underwear, a shaving bag, a notebook, envelopes, and stamps, and six books: *My Man Jeeves*, *In the Penal Colony*, a dictionary, *The Mark of Zorro*, *The Valley of Fear*, and *The Good Soldier*. There. I had done it, like he'd asked. How long was he going to stay, I wondered? I hoped. Right there in this cabin, I found the hope he was looking for.

"Unroll your dungarees," he said.

"No," I said softly.

"Please." Tommy stood, finally, and crossed his arms in gentle admonishment.

I slowly unrolled my dungarees to reveal a small wooden box. I set the box cleanly on the table and stood back, as if I were presenting it. I gestured to it.

"Open it, please."

"You already know what's in it, Tommy."

"I do," he said. "But I want you to show me."

I lifted the lid on the wooden box, my M1911 sidearm. With Tommy's bullet in the chamber.

"Rest? This is not rest." Tommy started towards me.

I began to cry, heavily. I leaned on the table, staring at the gun. Tommy put his hand on my back. At that moment, I did not fear him and his glowing eyes, or the woods outside, or the falling. He held me for a while. His warm eyes enrobing me and letting me fall apart within his hands.

"I don't want to die, Tommy."

"We've died already," he said. "We died along with those men among us, except our bodies and our souls got to come home. But our minds stay there. We walk about like a living dead. Our souls filthy and bruised and disgusting and capable of many horrible things. Our bodies keep ticking away the hours and minutes. Hours and minutes those men would kill again for right now. That their families would give anything for right now. It's our minds that keep us dead. Our minds keep us wishing we were already. Wishing we'd never gone, that we'd never seen what we'd seen. Wishing in and out of time."

Like a man who's figured out the meaning of life. Tommy let go to look at my face. My tears had wet his cheek, and they dried like a puddle in the sun against his eyes.

"You don't have to die, Greg. But you do have to decide what you want to do. Do you want to remember all of it?"

"I want to remember you," I said.

"All of that comes with me. You will have to stop falling too fast. The falling will never go away."

"I know, they said," I whispered.

"Well, I say, enjoy your soup and bread and beans and coffee with me. And we can make this falling a pleasant one." Tommy clapped his hands on the table in contentment.

"Have I been falling this whole time?" I was incredulous.

"Yes, you have, Greg. Is this something you can manage?"

"Yes. Yes, I think so." I gathered some pots and rinsed them thoroughly as Tommy talked about his days as a child. I'd found some aged ale under the cupboard and drank that heartily. We ate and drank and laughed by the fire. I grew tired and Tommy helped my sagging and giggly body to bed, then he left. I sat up and watched him through the window. The lights flickering through the wood, and then gone. One blink and it was morning.

I'd been gazing at the ceiling for hours, finally electing to sit up and begin the day. I let my gaze fall upon the two bowls and two cups of ale and smiled.

The sun peeked through the window. I dressed and put on my boots and coat and went down the haphazard path he'd led me on last night. My feet walked on with a mind of their own. And then I stopped. I stopped at a pair of hiking boots jutting out of the snow. The arm of a red jacket and a gloveless hand. And I knew. There he lay. For how long, I don't know. I don't know why but I brushed the snow off his face. Most of it gone at the site of the wound, near the temple. The edges of his face chewed away by something small. He was stiff and very cold, his expression almost angelic and serene. Not like MacArthur at all.

I went back to the cabin and grabbed my blanket. I placed it over his body and pegged down the four corners as best I could with nails I found on top of the hearth. I said a prayer. I'm not sure if I got the words correct, but it was the most religious experience

I'd had in my life. I walked slowly back to the cabin, looking back at the blanket every now and again.

That night I struggled to wash the bowls and ale cups. Not wanting to wash him away again. I swallowed hard, opened the front door, and poured the remnants of the dishes in the snow. The animals would be grateful. A warmth trickled onto my shoulders.

"I hope you've got something better than those beans tonight," Tommy said.

I grinned and he followed me back inside. I began to clean up and set the fire for dinner. Tommy began to hum.

"That song!" I shouted. "What is that?"

"Alexander's Ragtime Band," Tommy said with a smile.

"I thought about it yesterday. Made me sad."

Tommy grimaced. "Ah. You don't remember."

"I suppose not." I shrugged and brought two steaming bowls to the table.

"They were playing it as we entered the parade. Our pinkies touched on the float, and you smiled, and I smiled, then you scowled, and that was that."

"I do remember, I'm sorry, Tommy." I couldn't look up. Such a moment for us, for me. One I replayed almost every day since he disappeared.

"It's alright, Greg."

"How long will you stay?" I asked, still terrified to look at him.

"As long as you need."

"Is this falling? Will I be alright?" I finally looked up at him.

"You will live, that's what matters."

"Alright," I said and poured snow-chilled ale into our two mugs.

I wrote to Kastor and Sons the next day and resigned. The roads cleared out and I discovered a quaint tiny town in need of a librarian. So, I applied. Before I even left the interview, they offered it to me. It's the best job I've ever had. I headed back into the city for my things, never stopped to look about, or have a drink. Just kept going. When spring thaw came, I buried Tommy and placed a makeshift head stone for him.

He thanked me. And it was finally somewhat quiet in my mind. The kaleidoscope faded further each week.

Now, I'm a quiet, falling man, in a quiet town, in a quiet job. Rest. Tommy and I have sat and had many dinners over many years, many fires, and many drinks. I've had modern furniture delivered, and a radio, and more dishes, and wine, and full-priced meat in the icebox, and I'm quite fine indeed.

"You've outdone yourself tonight, Greg." Tommy smiled softly.

"Ah. It's come out just awful but you're kind enough."

"It's quite fine." Tommy sipped his wine slowly. "It's all quite fine, isn't it?"

"How do you mean?" I nervously pushed my underdone pot pie around on my plate. I knew what he was getting at. He'd hinted at it increasingly at every meal. How "fine" everything was. The meal, my job, my disposition mostly. He was leaving me.

"It's alright to let go, Greg. You've done well." Tommy pushed his wine away.

"I suppose it is, Tommy. I suppose it is." I reached for my glass of wine as a slight shadow cast upon the table, leaving its bulk on the empty chair opposite mine.

I was incredibly sad of course, but I understood. I needed to stop falling and start living. Dead or not. Filthy soul and atrocities done, I needed to get on with things—and I did for a short while. But things come back to haunt you out of nowhere, and the Tommys of the world caught between here and God knows where can't save you anymore. Can't stop you from spinning the barrel with the singular bullet that's been floating in the chamber for twenty-five years.

And as I age, I see the new boys going to war, a senseless one like they all are, and I pray they come home whole. I pray if not, that they have a Tommy. And then I pray they don't need one. But they always do. We always will. And if you look close enough, past our pleasant exteriors and cheerful demeanors, you might hear the wicked sound of our falling.

Wrath

There was a time when I thought: what a pity, a shame, an injustice. Murder, whether it be most foul or most deserved, is a heinous thing. A thing of challenged men, weak men, men who had lost their way. But now, as I perform my ritual: hot hand soak, nailbrush, nail file, three washes, one exfoliation and two pumps of sanitizer—I realize that blood on your hands can be relieving. Like unleashing a tightness. Carving out a space to breathe. I find that I quite like it. I find that I am obsessed with finding the justice in it.

Am I weak? Have I lost my way?

No.

Am I challenged? Indefinitely.

—Anonymous

In the Interest of Time

The low mewling and whimpering of a man swirled in the air of a windowless space. A space too clean and too virtuous to be housing an amply bleeding man chained to the floor, with one eye swollen shut. A man in black patrolled him in a semi-circle, his steely cold eyes gauging the broken man's pain. He cocked his head to the side and assessed a wound on the whimpering man's left cheek that seemed to bubble with every heaving breath, like a heartbeat, or the second hand of a watch.

Jacob Scale watched the whimpering man for several minutes with no movement, just a simple stare, causing the man to urinate in fear. He paced the room, at times stopping to kneel at the whimpering man's feet. The man shook his head violently and screamed as he pushed back against the wall. Jacob stood.

"Julia Mahan." Jacob spoke flatly.

"I told you, I don't know her!" The whimpering man coughed, splattering blood near his shoes.

Jacob grabbed the chain from the floor and tightened it around the man's legs, forcing out a terrible howl.

"Now, that's not entirely true, and I think we both know that. Have you become so jaded in your hobby you can no longer put a name to a face?" Jacob looked troubled and turned his back toward the whimpering man. The man heaved a heavy sigh, grateful to break the gaze.

"I don't look at faces."

Jacob approached a tall bench laid with knives in intricate shapes. He chose a long boning knife with a forked tip and stroked it gently. "Do you look at bodies?"

"Of course I look at bodies." The whimpering man tried to blink his bad eye as he squinted upward at Jacob. "Small, large. I look."

"How many is that now? Ten? Eleven?" Jacob turned back to the man, the knife gleaming under the stark fluorescent lights of the dark grey room. "Stephanie?" He tapped the knife against his palm. "Helena."

Tap.

"Monica."

Tap.

"Sarah."

"Jesus Christ, man!" The whimpering man twisted against his chains.

"Jennifer, Tessa, Donna, Patrice, Andrea, Amanda, and Julia. Were you going for an even dozen?"

"Let me out of here, man, I swear to God I won't fucking say anything, I swear to God, man!" The whimpering man's mouth hung agape and spilled its drool and blood mix down his sweat-soaked shirt.

"Well, we won't be doing that." Jacob surveyed the sight of the man, his restraints proved fine enough. He was pleased and let the corners of his mouth curl.

"Look, I know you man, people like you don't do shit like this, you're fucking crazy!" The whimpering man pulled against his chains, making him wheeze.

"Don't we? Don't we try to rid the world of evil things? Try to find the beauty in all things terrible? Now this, my dear man"—he pointed to the man's restraints with the forked knife—"is a thing of beauty. What you see here is a brief re-creation of the event. Now, I know I'm a bit unconventional in my methods, but I'm just trying to get the full picture here. You said, in your famous video during your incarceration, that first you chained them up." Jacob knelt on one knee in front of the whimpering man. "Would you say my work is similar to your craftsmanship?"

The whimpering man spat blood in Jacob's direction. "Fuck you!"

"It was a very simple question from one man trying to understand another man." Jacob yanked at the chain again, sending the man into a growl.

"Yes! Yes! It's the same. It's the same." The whimpering man muttered and sobbed.

"'And they may come to their senses.' Perfect. Now we've covered 'Bind,' let's move onto 'Torture.'" Jacob returned to the tall table and replaced the boning knife. He set his sights on three tightly bound leather parcels. Methodically, he unfastened each one to reveal a pristine set of metal dissecting tools.

"What are you gonna do?" the whimpering man asked in panic as his fingers trembled uncontrollably.

"Well, I would think explaining that point to you would be moot, considering your circumstances. I believe you know very well what I intend to do." Jacob paid great attention to his tools; he looked them over almost adoringly, like watching carefree children play in the yard from the second story window. He picked the first one up and scrutinized it, rubbing a slight smudge on a nearby linen.

"Look! I didn't mean to kill those girls, I don't usually do that, but I wasn't thinking. I was just—" The whimpering man began to spit and blubber. As he leaned forward, the chains tightened the binding, crushing his chest. He gasped and struggled to right himself.

Jacob grasped an ornate lancet, causing the whimpering man's eyes to widen in terror, and darted at the man, lithely slicing his good eye twice. "For we walk by faith, not by sight."

The man wailed and jerked against his restraints with such force he loosened his right wrist. Jacob hurriedly placed the tool back down and grabbed a ball mallet at the end of the tall table.

The whimpering man spat. "Please! Please! I won't tell anyone, I'll just go. You hear? You hear me? Are you still there?"

"Now correct me if I'm wrong ..." The whimpering man shot up at the sound and Jacob continued. "And speak up as the Lord has blessed me with only one working eardrum. You like to take the ladies out at the knees once you've tightly detained them, is that right?" Jacob asked. "Even if they got free, no running."

The whimpering man's head stayed down, he gagged loudly. Jacob banged the mallet on the cold stone floor. The clang reverberated like an echo in a silent church, shaking the instruments on the table.

"I repeat, is that right?" Jacob eyed the loose restraint.

"Yes. Yes." The whimpering man cried silently. The wails and spits gave way to a quiet understanding of his plight.

"Thank you. You see, I want to be as precise as I can." He patted the whimpering man's shoulder and continued. "I'm wanted upstairs in just a bit, so time really is of the essence, no hem or haw, just …" Jacob stood, and looked down at the whimpering and broken man who was now pallid and looking faint. "Just precision."

Jacob took a large step back and brought the mallet crashing down on the whimpering man's right knee, sending blood and flesh flinging, and exposing bones as if pushed free by his bawling scream. Without hesitation, he brought the mallet down on the man's left knee.

Winded, Jacob took a cloth from his chest pocket and wiped the mallet, setting it back against the tall instrument-laden table. He gazed at the whimpering man. "And then you cut the flexor tendons in their hands so that they couldn't grip?"

"Kill me, please." The whimpering man was a blend of anguish and catatonia, a vacant mass bubbling with terror and stupefied misery.

"Hush. Don't rush things. Low and slow, right, my child?"

"Kenneth."

"I'm sorry?" Jacob asked in surprise.

"You know my name is Kenneth."

"Strong Christian name." Jacob gripped his hands around two long scalpels and headed slowly back to the whimpering man. "Funny story about Christian names," Jacob began. "They have so many fables and rules about them. See this one, I think you'll like. The werewolf." Jacob chuckled to himself. "Now, hang on, I'm sure you're thinking, *now what is he after?* Well, in the seventeenth century, this little German valley had a rule. That if you saw a werewolf or any monstrosity, you simply had to address it by its Christian name three times and poof! No more werewolf, or what have you. Clean. Human again. Bye-bye Monster. Now what do you think will happen to you if we try that right now?"

"Please!"

"Patience, my friend." Jacob took a deep breath and sliced through the man's right hand, blood splattering on his dress slacks. "Kenneth!" he shouted.

Another slice to the left hand, the blow almost severing. The room now clouded with another howl from the whimpering man.

"Kenneth!" Jacob raised the whimpering man's incredibly pale and twisted face with the tips of the scalpels. "Kenneth!"

Crossing the two scalpels, he sliced the whimpering man's neck. Silence. No whimpering. No shriek.

Jacob worked methodically. First donning a heavy apron, boots, and goggles, he unchained the whimpering man, whose body slumped heavily to the basement floor with a thud. The checklist rattled in his brain. The heavy gloves were next, then rolling out the large thick-walled drum. Bend the body at all soft joints to submerge it into the drum. Mop thoroughly and scrub the wall. Remove the heavy gloves and apron, dispose of them in a long cardboard box. Nitrile gloves only and clean the tools with the green solution, not blue, and white cotton rag, toss in the cardboard box. Shine tools into their respective places in the leather-bound roll.

Jacob stepped into a tall shower box and scrubbed his hands and body vigorously, then stepped into a closet filled with black clothing in plastic dry cleaner bags. In an undershirt and underwear, Jacob donned a black shirt, black slacks, socks, and shoes. He pulled on another set of nitrile gloves and picked up his previous garments and tossed them into an incinerator with the long cardboard box. Clean. Human again.

Jacob headed up several flights of stairs to enter the street level. He looked up to the sun and inhaled slowly, a slight smile on his lips. His gaze traveled down to a happy nuclear family waving at him from across the street.

Jacob Scale, human, private citizen, child of God. He gingerly punched a code on a nearby door and was greeted by a woman with a warm smile.

"Good morning, Linda."

"Service starts in ten minutes, I was getting worried. Your coffee is lukewarm." She smiled at him.

Jacob returned her smile, tenderly. "So sorry, I had a little spill I had to clean up and lost my sense of time."

"I'm making another pot," said Linda. He motioned to help but was shooed away.

"Tell me, Linda, did any of the families of those women respond?"

"Yes, they'll be meeting with you today after the service. Ms. Mahan just this morning decided to come."

Jacob clutched his hands together and held them to his heart. "That's lovely news."

"Yes, she's had the longest to mourn. Julia being the first." Linda headed to a tall closet and retrieved a small white box. "Those poor girls. I can't believe they let that monster free after what he did to them. *Circumstantial.* Just obscene." Linda's head shook swiftly in disbelief.

Jacob straightened his spine. "I can't either. But 'God is our refuge and strength, a very present help in trouble.' We will free those families from pain as best we can."

Linda came behind him and opened the white box. With great esteem, she placed his cleric collar on and reached back into the tall closet for a white cassock.

"Yes, Father, as best we can."

Envy

I go to sleep and wake with the same feeling. Just once, I'd like you to want for something. Just once. It's a nail in the coffin every time you win, or score, or get profiled, get fawned over and I can't stomach it one more day. I dream of you falling far and fast, hitting hard. I think about hiring someone to put you out of your misery. I think about staging a car crash. I think about it all. Every day. And every day you wake and sit four feet from the finish line and watch all of us losers straggle up behind as you blithely cross over it. One day, it'll all happen the way I need it to. One day.

—Collin Auberon (Orange Moleskine, 2014)

Free Weight

Chapter One: Secret Sauce and Shit Sandwiches

Collin Auberon sat lazily in his chair, his hand bent awkwardly through a shock of jet-black hair with a white streak running through it as if it were on the lam. His fingers absent-mindedly stroked the mouse of his computer as it hovered over an urgent email from Jim Handler, agent extraordinaire. Jim Handler was once referred to by Penguin Publishing's out-going president in 1996 as a "shit-sandwich," but Collin loved him just the same. His eyes darted quickly to a disgusting-looking dish being made on the local tv morning show.

A cell phone vibration shook Collin out of his stupor. He tapped the speaker feature and readied himself for the blow.

"If we don't get higher on this list, we're gonna lose our leverage for percentage." Jim Handler's gruff voice was even and calculated. "What the hell's going on?"

"Hello to you too, Jim." Collin closed the email. No sense answering now.

"Don't fuck with me, kid. That son of a bitch is killing us."

"Yeah, I saw it, Jim. I'm down four slots. Still NYT Best Seller territory, though. You gotta hand it to me."

"But Bramwell's got a secret sauce though. You gotta find your own. It's been ten years of this dicking around, kid." Jim rarely addressed Collin as the forty-seven-year-old man he'd become. Jim, only fifty, always fancied himself the Mickey to Collin's Rocky and it was fucking exhausting.

Picking up the newspaper again to study the list, Collin heaved another sigh. He grimaced at the distance between his name and Stephen Bramwell. A thorn in Collin's side, figuratively and literally. Bramwell had cost him money, status, sweat, and depression. There was something otherworldly about him. A giant in stature, with this odd Mother Theresa mentality that never really sat well with Collin. *No one's that good and honorable. Everyone's got an angle.*

Bramwell being twenty years his senior, Collin had grown up with him and to Collin, he was a horror god. He simply had to read every book, short story, and article Stephen Bramwell had ever released. His first ever fan fiction was based on Due Sellers, a cocaine-addicted detective in Bramwell's third horror novel *Dead Inside*. He'd cut the typing paper in half and gingerly set it horizontally in the typewriter, creating a small book by the end of it. Four chapters in total. Due Sellers had a new life, loves—well, several, but mostly just sex—and a whole lot of blood on his hands. He wrote to Bramwell one summer on a whim. The new Due was too good to waste on classmates like Richie Festa and Henry Eddard. He had to let Bramwell know the work he'd continued so deftly. He cautiously pulled the staples out of issue one of Due: Private Detonation and headed to Todd's Copies. A pristine new copy of Collin's prized novelette headed to his idol that day.

Summer came and went, and so did young Collin's energy for anything Due—or Bramwell for that matter. He hadn't even received a canned response from Bramwell's publisher, and Henry Eddard died tragically a few weeks before. *Under Foot: Tales from Six Feet Deep* by Stephen Bramwell released in July of that year and Collin still hadn't picked it up, turned it over, or even browsed the description until a telegram arrived that evening during dinner.

Collin—
Whoa! I love what you've done with Due here! I guess I better watch my back. Keep up the good work, kid!
—Stephen Bramwell

And that was that. Fuck Due. Fuck fan fiction. He could do it. On his own, with his own ideas. A star was born in 1984. Sort of.

"Kid! Kid!" Jim was shouting.

"Huh?" Collin licked his lips, he was drooling.

"Are you even on this planet?" Jim's throaty bellow broke him out of his daze. "We've got some junkets in LA, San Diego, and Boston this month. Make it happen."

"Will do, Jim. We'll put the shine on." Collin stood and stretched, flopping the paper down again.

"Oh! One more thing, kid."

"Whoa! Jim, hang on."

Collin's attention was turned by a female newscaster's inflection of a name on the low-volume television.

The screen filled with the ultra-flattering and ever-present picture of Stephen Bramwell that had graced the back of his books for over fifteen years. Bramwell looked jovial leaning against a brick wall. The news chyron didn't match that sentiment.

"Writing such thriller novels as *The Grassland Girls*, *It Only Comes at Night*, and *Low Hanging Fruit*, Stephen Bramwell has been scaring the world for decades. So, it's no surprise the amount of sorrow coming from the literary world today as we learn Stephen has stage four lung cancer."

A short montage of Stephen Bramwell flooded the screen, signing autographs peppered with family vacations.

"Jesus fucking Christ." Collin dropped the remote on the cell phone out of shock.

"The fuck are you doing, kid?"

"Jim, hang on! Jesus!" Collin raised the volume to a shout.

"It's not known when Stephen Bramwell was diagnosed, as the family just released a statement today and asks for privacy and respect at this time. Such a sad, sad story. After this short break we'll be back with weather on the—"

Collin switched the television off, frozen in a moment of fear and possibility. He shut off the speaker and raised the phone to his ear.

"Jim, did you catch any of that?"

Jim's response was muffled by a mouthful of something. "Nah. Something wrong?"

Collin unconsciously rubbed his chin. "Maybe not. Could you get me in touch with Bramwell's agent?"

"You thinking about jumping ship?" Jim's wet chewing continued.

"Hardly. I'm gonna find out what's in the sauce. Bramwell's dying."

A slight watery choke. "Say what?"

"Jim, I said Bramwell is dying. I'm gonna see if he's got any sage advice for me before it's all over."

"You're a sick sonofabitch, kid."

Collin hung up first. He ran his hands down his face and sat in silence. A buzz on his desk sent the newspaper scurrying. Bramwell's agent, Marcia. Collin picked up quickly.

"Hello?"

"Hi Collin, Marcia Bienza. Jim Handler told me you requested to speak with me. I don't have much time as you know, it's gonna be a bit crazy today."

"Of course, yes, thank you so much for reaching back out, um I—um …" Collin scrambled for a pen on his mess of a desk. "I was wondering if you could arrange a lunch between Stephen and me. I'd really like to see him."

"Oh, I might, Collin. I'll see if he's up to it. Hold please."

"Oh! Oh sure."

Soft muzak came across the line: Christopher Cross, *Arthur's Theme*. Collin bopped along. Just as he opened his mouth to sing, Marcia returned.

"Could you see Stephen at home, say tomorrow at noon?"

"In Connecticut?"

"Yes, in Darien. I could arrange a hotel for you, Mr. Auberon."

Collin was stunned and rushed and grateful and stupefied—but oddly settled, self-assured. He'd finally be able to tap the master, to drain a bit of essence. The thought made Collin sick. But desperate men do desperate things. Mad things.

"That'd be just fine, Marcia, I'll head out of San Francisco tonight."

"I'll send you reservations through Jim, it'll come via Denise Manello, my assistant. Safe travels, Mr. Auberon."

"Thank you, Marcia." Collin's lips parted as the words of praise and sportsmanship threatened to flow out of his mouth like a broken dam. Click. Dial tone.

"Well damn."

Erin wasn't gonna be happy about this.

Erin Auberon wasn't happy about much these days, and she'd always had a low grumbling for Stephen Bramwell. He bested Collin at every turn, on every best seller roster. She started off coy, teasing Collin about it, hoping it would rouse him into better work. Slowly it began to fester, as if Bramwell was keeping her from a better life. Better friends, better status, better bragging rights. Erin soon began to resent Collin for her station, being married to the second banana didn't look good for the social event invites she almost salivated upon hoping to receive but didn't. That lack of status—and Collin's extra forty pounds hadn't done much to sweeten the deal either.

During their last intimate encounter, Erin looked like she was waiting for an hour-late bus, and she'd asked him to keep his shirt on.

Collin's first five years in the author space were electric, he was the new hotshot wunderkind. Forty pounds lighter. Thirty and thriving. He'd had his share of actresses by then, had a social cocaine habit, and was even invited to Rod Stewart's album release party in the Hollywood Hills. That's where he'd met a stage actress named Erin O'Reilly. They'd made unabashed love in several closets before heading to the brush along the mile long driveway. Six weeks later, Erin was pregnant and, with a push from Jim on image, he'd asked Erin to quietly tie the knot in Carmel-by-the-Sea. Eight months later, Ethan was born. He spent the next four years playing spooky dad: letting Ethan meet Alice Cooper and Tom Savini, showing him scary special effects—desperately trying to hang on to that bad boy edge with a side of endearing father. Endearing husband was never the game. Of course, the women still reached out, whom he obliged for company—and the occasional ego and otherwise stroke. Erin let it slip to the press about her unhappiness.

Collin churned out a novel a year, was always busy, was always entertaining. Four months later, Erin was pregnant with Owen. Ah, the industry spin. Everyone is happy.

Collin packed the necessities. Two casual outfits, one suit just in case—a black one. A morbid color choice, but Collin stifled any guilt. He set off down the stairs, nearly tripping face forward over a lacrosse stick.

"God dammit, Ethan, get this thing out of here!" No response, a quiet house. A bright yellow post-it hung on the front door.

"Thanks for helping me carry Owen's science project to school today, asshole."

Collin grabbed a pen off the entry desk and scribbled at the bottom of the note.

"You're welcome!"

He used his suitcase to push through the door and locked it.

Chapter Two: The Drain

Collin's stride was flat-footed and dazed as he groggily strolled through Westchester County Airport, his eyes pink from rough sleep in a windy sky. As he scanned the airport terminal for the livery sign, he cocked his head at the stout man holding a sign bearing AUBERON. The man sighed and stepped forward.

"Collin Auberon?" A lifeless driver in an ill-fitting captain's hat beckoned flatly.

"Yessir."

"Right this way."

No "Hey aren't you …?", no "Oh, wow I've read …!" Just another fare in the wee hours of the morning. *Just as well, not in the mood for autographs anyway.*

Collin stared at the small black-and-white picture of Bramwell in the newspaper shoved into the backseat of the cab. He lifted it slowly to his eyes, trying to make out the story in the sporadic streetlight.

"You like his books?"

"Hmm? Oh yes, very much so." Collin nodded: eyes wide, eager to cut the coldness.

The driver scoffed. "I can't get into horror books. Too many bad dreams after, I sleep too little as it is. He's dying, right?"

"Oh Bramwell? Yes, unfortunately. You know we're writing riv—"

"Have you heard about the extortions?" The driver continued undisturbed.

Collin swallowed his irritation at the interruption. "Extortions? No!"

"Yeah, yeah." The driver spoke to Collin in the rearview mirror. "People trying to get money out of him, sue him like he stole their stories, shit like that. Shame. Can you imagine trying to drain a dying guy like that? Sheesh. Only in America."

"Fuck," Collin whispered.

"I'm sorry, Mr. Auberon?"

"No, yes, only in America." Setting the paper on the seat next to him, he absent-mindedly stroked it and sank into the seat, satisfied to drive in silence the rest of the way.

"W Hotel on your left." The driver's voice stunned a sleeping Collin awake.

He rubbed his eyes and searched nervously around for the paper that had fallen to the car floor.

"Ah, yes, thank you!" Collin shuffled swiftly out of the car.

The driver popped the trunk and Collin stared at him in silence, watching him tally something on a clipboard, still sturdily within the driver's seat. Collin departed, grabbed his suitcase and meekly walked over to hand the driver a twenty-dollar bill.

"Safe travels back home, Mr. Auberon."

Before Collin responded, the black livery cab sauntered off into the night. Collin headed to the hotel entrance with heft, almost blown there by a gusty summer wind.

On the plane, Collin had taken in the first six chapters of Stephen Bramwell's newest novel *Low Hanging Fruit*, a terror-filled account of a killer on a rampage during the 1930s jazz era. Bramwell loved jazz. He found that out when they shared a few drinks at Cabbage Head, a basement level watering hole near NYU when Collin was working on his MFA. Bramwell had come to his lecture hall that day to speak about structure. Collin flagged him down across a crowded hall at the close of class by shouting, "Hey! Read anything good lately like *Due: Private Detonation?*"

Bramwell beamed and invited him for a drink. They talked for hours about horror films, old girlfriends, friends that had passed away from something stupid or their own hand, how both of their fathers had pulled the old "going out for smokes" trick and never returned. From hero to friend.

"Hey." Collin nudged a then forty-year-old Bramwell in the arm. "Can you take a look at this? Tell me where I'm missing something?"

Collin pulled a bright yellow folder out of his backpack and handed it to Bramwell.

"The hell is it?" Bramwell opened and thumbed the papers inside.

"It's the first pages of my novel, *Standing Tall in the Grasslands*. It's like *Children of the Corn* but like, these little girls have been raised in this incredibly tall grass all their lives and they don't know that the world is anything else and when developers come to make room for condos, it unleashes a demonic force that's been protecting these girls from other humans."

"For what?" Bramwell sipped at the brown liquor in the beveled tumbler, his fourth.

"What?" Collin was stunned.

"From what? Like, why are they being protected?"

"Shit, Stephen, I have no idea." Collin and Stephen both laugh.

"Well, that's what you're missing. But I'll take a look and see if I find anything else." Bramwell raised his glass and Collin enthusiastically clinked his too hard and chipped it.

"Shit, really? Man, thanks!"

That October, Bramwell released his newest thriller, *The Grassland Girls*. Collin stood feverish with anger at the large poster in the Waldenbooks on 110th Street. He bounded inside and grabbed the first copy he could, flipped it over and shot twenty dollars at the clerk and didn't wait for change. He sat down across the street and opened the first pages to a dedication page and there, staring him down, was the first line of his novel.

"Like a sparkling Sedona sunset that reached out before her, it was all there, all the colors melting into one. She was new. Unseen before by these new folk."

—For Due

That sonofabitch. Collin read on. It was gorgeously terrifying. Every phrase, every shock. And nothing like his original story. Collin closed the book as the reading light faded and headed home. Bramwell had morphed and stolen his title, that was for sure. But he'd inspired the man, that was also for sure. And in good ol'

American pissing contest fashion, Collin's first novel *Cherry Pits*, an absolute smash out of the gate, addressed its dedication:

To the buyers and sellers, watch your back.

And there it began, a low bubbling friction. Bramwell had shown Collin how to turn on the world and placed it in his fourteen-year-old hands to blossom. And now he was going to bleed him dry for whatever inspiration he had left.

Chapter Three: Windows to the Soul

The drive to the Bramwell home, its thin streets parted by tree-lined medians, made Collin all the more anxious. He'd met Stephen over a hundred times. The ball-busting banter, a slap on the back from Stephen's catcher's-mitt-sized hands. Easy.

Snarky, but easy.

He expected some pretentious, architectural compound, not a smart, white colonial style home nestled far from the road in the middle of minivan paradise. Much more space than his and Erin's tight and rapidly-aging three floor Queen Anne in San Francisco.

On the well-manicured grounds of the Bramwell home, taking in the meticulous design of the florals, the ground cover, the trees, Collin was still confused by the softness of it all in comparison to Bramwell's Vonnegut-like brashness. The left corner of the lawn, a deep blue variety of flowers that melted almost seamlessly to a violet then to a remarkable yellow. Like a Sedona sunset.

Damn.

"He's good, isn't he?" Andrea Bramwell smiled at the sprawling wildflowers.

Collin spun, marveled by her soft tone and furthermore, her gentle admiration for her husband.

"He had those flowers planted the year we bought the house. *The Grassland Girls* came first. I just try my best to do him proud by keeping them up." She stretched out her hand. "Andrea Bramwell, nice to meet you, Collin."

"Andrea, yes, thank you, so sorry, I was just taken by the landscaping. You've done a really excellent job here."

"Easy now, we just paid for it, honey, I didn't dig 'em. Come on inside, we are expecting you." Andrea Bramwell stood eye to eye with 6' 2" Collin, dripping in Lululemon and a warm smile.

"Absolutely lovely for you to visit Stephen, Collin. It's nice to see someone arrive without a camera attached to their shoulder."

"The press hounding you? At this moment?"

"Them and everyone else."

"That's fucking terrible, Andrea." Collin flung his hand to his mouth, giving a gentlemanly decorum her essence seemed to reach down and pull out of him.

"Ha! It's ok to say that. It is fucking terrible." She shouted ahead, "Honey? Collin's here!"

The Bramwell home's cathedral ceilings seemed to go up for miles, most likely to compensate for Stephen's height.

Andrea led Collin through to a skinny set of French doors opening into a great room with a wall of windows. Collin turned red and swallowed hard. An incredible view of the water with the rain tapping. Light Tchaikovsky played in the background. *Of course it did.*

Stephen Bramwell, all sixty-seven years and six feet, seven inches of him, stood opposite an easel. His body was concave, features angular, cheekbones like a 17th century patriarch.

"He paints?" Collins scoffed, half amazed, half irritated.

"Yes. Badly." Andrea let Collin continue through on his own.

Bramwell turned with warmth in his eyes as he set sight upon Collin. Half the weight Collin remembered, and he tried his best to keep the shock from his face but failed miserably. Collin stepped forward, hand outstretched.

"Stephen."

"Collin. So nice of you to come."

The men shook briskly. Collin let go first but caught something flashing in Stephen's eyes. Pain, then relief.

"Of course. How're you holding up?" Collin's legs were lead. Still amazed at Bramwell's waifish build.

"Eh, here and there a bad moment. I don't really leave this room for much anymore."

"It's lovely, Stephen." Collin counted the panes, more than his whole first level at home.

"The view helps—and that view." Stephen pointed at Andrea in the doorway.

"I'll leave you boys to it." Andrea closed one French door.

Jesus, he looks terrible. Collin finally stepped forward.

"I'm so sorry, Stephen."

Stephen gently stepped back from the easel, taking stock of his mess of abstract nothingness.

"Ah, don't be. You play the cards you're dealt." A disturbing cough broke the pleasantries. Stephen hunkered over, waving off any help from a panicked Collin.

"Jesus! Should I get Andrea?"

Stephen finally took a long inhale. "Nah, she knows the difference between a tickle and a call to 911. Come. Sit." Stephen pointed to two tufted chairs facing the window wall. The view was even more glorious head on.

Stephen slowly lowered into the chair. The fabric, the style, even the tufting all dwarfed the man's frame in comparison.

"So," Stephen began. "What brings you?"

"I just wanted to say, the rivalry. It's been a ride. You're a hell of a writer, Stephen."

"I never saw us as a rivalry. I know I'm a hell of a lot better than you."

Collin scratched his neck, almost guarding his jugular, and sank deep into the chair.

"Ah." Collin coughed loudly.

Stephen chuckled. "What I mean is that I was stronger structurally, your work is guttural and raw. I mean, you beat the shit out of Due and I loved it. We're just so different. It's press that made us rivals. Good for business."

Yeah, the press.

Collin wanted to run the hell out of there as fast as he could. Bramwell didn't give a shit about a rivalry. He knew Collin was good in his own way. The End. Period.

"Well, you've whooped my ass sales-wise these last three years. Where the hell did that come from?" Collin covered his mouth in embarrassment. That question bared more teeth than it needed to. After all, he was here for the secret sauce, the drain, and right now there wasn't that big of a difference between being an ass and acting like one.

You filthy, dirty bastard. Here you sit, gazing at flowers, his home, his wife. You're trying to compete with a husk, now, you know that, Collin?

Collin shook his head. Stephen's buzzsaw voice droned in his ears. How long had Stephen been speaking? Collin didn't know. He blinked twice then began to follow along. Stephen's eyes grew distant for a few moments. Gazing out at the water, his eyes widened and shut.

"Sometimes life calls you to right the wrongs, the little twinges of shit that tough times kick up, the shit you wanna forget. Or didn't wanna deal with. All the things you swore you'd never tell anyone or the things you hoped folks forgot. It all came out at once, like a flood."

Collin crossed his arms, letting his elbows fall on the well-padded armrests. "The payback. Is that what you think this diagnosis is?"

"Nah, that came later, coincidentally when I had righted the ship, so to speak."

Stephen shifted in his seat uncomfortably, never taking his eyes off the water. Collin followed suit and stared ahead. Trying hard to see whatever had captured Stephen.

"Aria and Angie turned sixteen that year." Stephen's voice was wet. He cleared his throat heartily.

"Bless you for raising twin girls, couldn't have been easy. It's hard enough for me with two boys five years apart."

"Shit, I'm not done yet." A small chuckle leaves Stephen, his face returns quickly to frightened wonder. "As I said, they turned sixteen that year. Everything was loud, obnoxious, overly noxious, in tears, in makeup. It was all a bit much, times two. God bless Andrea. I don't know how she did it, but I'm sure the wine-of-the-week club helped."

"As it should," Collin chirped.

Stephen continued. "I was banging my head against a wall trying to produce a new idea or several. A breakthrough that I could meld into a dozen stories and with the dangly bits of terror I usually give. But nothing. Dry."

"I can't imagine that for you. Me? It's like betting against the sun coming up the next day." Collin shifted his gaze back to a mesmerized Stephen. The rain was heavier yet still soft against the mile-high panes of glass.

"I had to leave. I love my daughters, but I needed time away."

"A vacation is always a clever idea." Collin hadn't noticed that he'd completely shifted his body toward Stephen.

"It started off as a vacation but became something bigger, stronger. A pull to leave."

Something in Stephen's tone pricked the hairs on the back of Collin's neck. Stephen rose to a stand. Collin jumped up as Stephen swayed and was waved away again. Collin sat back down heftily, like a scolded child, as Stephen approached the wall of windows.

"I purchased a cabin about a decade ago, for us. We'd only gone as a family once and then I think we kind of just forgot we had it. Didn't even sublet."

"Where at?" Collin leaned forward a bit, elbows on his knees, his head propped between his fists, at his idol's feet once again.

"Carmel-by-the-Sea, right near Big Sur."

"Oh nice! Gorgeous place."

"It was at first. Six miles away from any other cabin, good solace. I needed that space."

"So, it was worth it?"

Stephen's eyes gazed around the water, as if searching for something. "In ways. The fresh air felt great. Powerful even though it was heavy. So, I unpacked and sat there and just let it come."

"What are the girls, now? Eighteen? That was a banner year for you. I guess it did come."

"Oh, it came. In droves. So hard it was difficult to know when to stop. When to say when, but eventually I did. *All is Well* was born and I came home."

"How long were you there?"

"Fifteen days."

Collin jumped to his feet and bounded over to Stephen. "Holy shit! You wrote *All is Well* in fifteen days?!"

"Yes. Yes, I did."

He's got to be putting me on.

A tall tale, right at the end, for posterity's sake. Stephen's eyes became troubled again as he moved gingerly from the window wall back to the chair. Collin didn't follow.

"And *It Only Comes at Night*, did you write that there too?"

"Yes."

"How long?"

"Ten days."

"Fuck me!"

"Indeed. It was the air." Stephen continued, "Everything touched you. The inspiration. It'll find you if you let it in. I wanted to be there more than here, like I said, it was a pull."

"So, all you had to do was let go of the shit, then? Hmm." A bewildered Collin leaned hard against the window wall and jolted back upright.

"In a way."

"That's phenomenal, Stephen. I don't even want to ask how long it took for this last one that's scaring the shit out of me."

Andrea popped in, startling Collin, whose knuckles cracked hard against the window.

"Shit! Sorry!"

"They're stronger than they look." She shot Collin an endearing smile before turning her attention to Stephen. "Stephen, honey, can I get you and Collin some tea? I was just going to put on another pot."

"Always, my birdie. Collin?"

Collin despised tea. The earthy water, the syrups and accoutrement that constantly fell on his face every time he opened a cupboard door at home. Erin was obsessed. *My God, do I really not like anything about her?*

"Of course, I'd love some, Andrea. Thank you." Andrea exited with a nod. Stephen turned his gaunt face to Collin for the first time in almost an hour.

"I'm glad you're here, Collin." Stephen sighed. "I'm never gonna see the trees turn again. Not here, not the redwoods, not Big Sur."

Collin gulped and headed back over to the chair beside Stephen. "Hey, we don't have to talk like that."

"Why the fuck not? You've given me an excellent idea. Would you like it?"

"Like what?"

"The cabin?"

"Wow! In Big Sur? Shit, Erin would go nuts! I'd love it but—" Collin looked down, defeated. His current book sales and soon-to-be-impending declination of sales due to Bramwell's diagnosis stopped the excitement.

"I'd have to check the finances, Stephen, I'd want to be fair to your asking price."

"I didn't ask if you wanted to buy it, I asked if you wanted it. I'm giving it to you."

"Why? Doesn't Andrea—"

"Andrea doesn't want a thing to do with that eye sore. Not since ..." Stephen trailed off.

"The diagnosis, sure. Sorry, Stephen."

Stephen's eyes gathered much more sorrow this time around. "It would definitely lessen the load around here. Let Andrea breathe without figuring out how to destroy that thing."

"Lots of issues with it?"

"Ha." Stephen chuckled. "I guess you could say that."

"Well, of course, Stephen. I'll take it off your hands for you."

Stephen reached out a shaky hand. The fingers longer, skin thinner and clammier than Collin expected. He was truly taking in Mr. Stephen Bramwell for the first time in fifteen years. Every line and crack, every sallow sag of yellowing skin, the steely blue-grey of his eyes which seemed to fog up in real time like cataracts. The idol was crumbling.

He fantasized about what Erin would say about the cabin, about taking her in every room of it, bringing some of that spark back. Collin's mind switched between guilt and desire, and it was giving him a migraine. He unwittingly began to pull at a thread in the chair fabric in restlessness.

"You're a good man, Collin."

"It's no trouble at all, my friend."

Friend. Collin meant it. A lilt in his stomach pulled him to sit straight. All the years wasted fighting a one-sided battle.

Andrea brought in two steaming mugs and set them on the small table between the men. She placed a long kiss on Stephen's head, his hair now a spiderweb, an echo of the bushy black pompadour for which he was famous. Stephen lifted the mug at Collin. Collin raised his in return.

"You're the only other author that's showed up." Stephen slowly sipped his tea. Collin cleared his throat softly and joined them in the viewing. Andrea slid her arms down Stephen's chest as they quietly stared at the rain and water. Silence. Love everlasting. Preoccupied, Collin spun his wedding band.

Imagine trying to drain a dying guy like that.

Chapter Four: Keys to the Kingdom

Collin lifted his carry-on out of the rental car and slammed the trunk. He'd taken the long way to the airport, he needed distraction, time to think. Collin had failed at his mission. Draining the secret sauce didn't seem to matter at this point. He'd gained a friend. Two, hopefully. He pleasantly daydreamed on his long drive about Stephen and Andrea meeting Erin, the boys meeting the twins, of laughing in the window room while Stephen beat all odds. He imagined Stephen getting his hair back. Erin and Andrea quietly gossiping and commiserating in the corner, their eyes looking on. He thought about Erin walking through a mid-century wooden hideaway, the way the corners of her mouth turned upward at the stories he'd tell at their dinner parties. Half proud, half shut the hell up already. He missed the playfulness about her. He'd missed a lot of things. He'd missed a great friendship, with a great man, all on account of optics. That was about to change.

An ill-tempered wheel on his suitcase took to rumbling in the concrete garage, alerting everything in its midst. A car alarm went off. A vibration from his chest surprised him, making him drop the suitcase. Collin pulled his cell phone out of his pocket.

"Jim? Jim, hang on." Collin rumbled back to the car for peace and quiet. "Jesus, sorry Jim. What's up?"

"Hey kid. How was your visit with Bramwell? Get your secret sauce?"

"It was oddly amazing. Really amazing. God, he looks rough, but his spirit was a lot kinder than I thought it would be. I'll have to reach out to him and Andrea when I get back."

"Yeah, well don't bother. He's dead."

"Dead?! I just saw him this afternoon!" Collin frantically checked his watch. 5:30 p.m.

"Died around two o'clock. Marcia said he'd requested another cup of tea and when his wife came back in, there he was, dead in his chair."

"I—"

"You there, kid?"

"Yes. My God, Andrea. The girls."

Collin began to cry. Somewhere deep within, in a fragment of a second, he imagined his own death. The lack of mourners, the look of stoic resignation on Erin's face. He thought about Henry Eddard's funeral and how he could barely hold in his breakfast and made a spectacle out of himself.

"Yeah, I don't know what this blubbering is all about, kid, but we have a junket in four days, so my suggestion—"

"I'm gonna stay. Until after the funeral."

"Excuse me?"

"I'm staying for the funeral, Jim. Cancel L.A."

"Kid!"

Collin hung up and tossed the cell phone and the luggage in the passenger side and drove out of the lot.

The crowd was modest at St. John's Catholic Cemetery that Wednesday, on the warmest day in weeks. A sea of black, bowed bodies, the occasional flash of a white handkerchief. The light buzz of a bumblebee hummed on the navy-blue flowers that grew near the head of the grave like an arbor. The Bramwell plot had been employed. Room for one more. Andrea stood, flanked by two red-faced, brunette daughters who had inherited their father's height. Her eyes were red. Her lips, pursed to stop the quivering. She stared straight at the coffin.

I wonder what she's telling him.

They seemed like the kind of couple who could speak volumes in a glance, in a small smattering of words. Maybe she was thanking him for his time. Maybe she was cursing him for leaving her alone, with two daughters on the verge of starting their own lives without her. Maybe she was thinking of her next move, a big move. Out of the beautifully landscaped haven with the wall of windows that looked out at a world without Stephen Bramwell. As the coffin lowered into the ground, Andrea broke her silence. The gasp and scream surprised no one, as if they'd all been waiting for her dam to break.

The crowd scatters and Collin made his way over to Andrea. She was alone, looking out into the distance.

"Andrea?"

She turned, brought out of her daydream. "Oh, Collin, yes. Thank you so much for staying here for him. That's so kind of you."

"Of course. He was a great man."

"My favorite." They both smile timidly to each other, half hoping the other would start to speak.

"I'm grateful to see you, I didn't want to mail this." Andrea reached into her clutch purse and pulled out an envelope. Balled up tissues streaked with makeup tumbled out in the shuffle. She gasped.

"Leave it." Collin laughed.

"Never. I threw a cola can out of Stephen's Chevy once in '79. He never let me forget it."

Collin scooped them up and handed them to her.

"So embarrassing." Andrea fiddled with the clasp on the clutch and gave up. "Here."

"What's this?"

"It's the keys to the cabin Stephen left you, and the instructions. He had me put them together as soon as you left. I had our groundskeeper Gary head out there and juice the generator for you."

"Jesus, I didn't think he was serious. Just the—"

"Ramblings of a dying man?"

"No. Oh God, no." Collin could feel the sweat on his back pooling near his waist band.

Andrea nodded. "Yes, it was. But honest ramblings. I can't thank you enough for taking it off my hands."

"Honestly, I'm grateful. He said it was a little rundown. Anything I should look out for to keep her going?"

Andrea's features took on a disgusted expression as she peered at the envelope in Collin's hands. Hatred. She let out a heavy sigh and took a deep inhale, then smiled. Almost too wide.

"Rundown is relative. It's what you want it to be."

Andrea shook Collin's free hand vigorously.

"Andrea, I'm so sorry for your loss."

Andrea began to weep, the smile never leaving her face. "For the world's."

She turned away from Collin and walked swiftly to meet the limousine. Collin placed the envelope in his suitcoat pocket. He felt an odd wind, too cool, on this 83-degree day. The gravediggers wasted no time getting the burial show on the road.

It had been a whirlwind for Collin, after touching back down in San Francisco. Everyone was still home where he'd left them. The boys were oblivious to his return and Erin was her usually sour self. After arranging a private dinner for just him and Erin, hoping to position his newly acquired cabin as a romantic getaway, a place to get back to square one, she had beaten him to the punch. She'd had time to think and gather the gumption. She timidly pushed her food around her plate.

"I've been to see Curtis. We've got the details worked out. I want the house and 30 percent. No more, no less. I think that's fair."

Collin sat there, watching her body deflate with the words, then inflate with confidence. She sank her knife into her steak and stared up at him.

"So?" she said.

Collin got up from the table and headed to the reception podium, paid the bill, and left, leaving Erin to happily cut her meat alone.

Chapter Five: Who's There

Collin drove along the road, pensive, half present and half back in Darien, in full argument with a harried Jim.

"You cannot blow off this entire junket, kid."

"Stop calling me kid, I hate it when you call me kid. We're two years apart. And I'm not blowing it off, I'm postponing. Besides, I'm up six places today."

"Look, Collin, in this business, a day is a week, a week is a month. We don't got that kind of time. We gotta keep this momentum going."

"Spin it, Jim. Author, distraught by the death of his colleague, takes a brief press hiatus. Stephen loved my writing. Especially *Cherry Pits*. Tell them that."

"What, you think Bramwell's rundown shack is gonna help you? How does Erin feel about you spending so much time in Bramwell land?"

"Well, she had me served with divorce papers a week after I landed, so I'd say she's pretty fine with it all. Jim, give me the weekend, I'll be in touch." He ended the call.

Collin's mouth dropped as he turned off the wooded pathway to a brown steel-sided A-frame. "This can't be it." Collin looked at his instructions again. "Yep, Red Owl Hideaway. Run down my ass."

The cabin looked to have been carved straight from the wood. Collin could understand the attraction to the place. The exterior was a thing of beauty. A carport, about twenty feet from a small walking bridge that abutted the house, had chiseled ornate trim work. A jack-o-lantern face of windows greeted him.

"Fuck me, you're beautiful."

Collin grabbed his suitcase and rolled it onto the porch, that ornery wheel catching between two planks. He grunted and then left it, heading back to the car for his backpack, four bags of food and an eighteen pack of beer. Labored with the baggage, he grappled with the keys in the envelope. Three locks, easy turns.

The cabin sang with that sweet blend of moss-eaten air and damp time-forgotten furniture.

"Hello?" Collin shouted and shook his head. "Idiot." He closed the door behind him, gently.

"Honey, I'm home! This place is cherry. What the hell was he talking about?" He flipped all four switches on the front panel and in a cascade the first-floor rooms are flooded with light.

Collin placed the food and beer away in their respective places and checked for dishes and silverware. The place was a dream. Nature sounds abounded as Collin sat at the large oak desk in the corner of the room and ran his finger along a strange carving in the desk: *write the wrongs.*

"Ah. Cheeky, Stephen." Collin clapped his hands. "Let's fire it up." Breaking out his go-to orange canvas-bound notebook from his backpack, he creased the spine for a new page and lifted the lid of his laptop, slyly rubbing his hands together. Collin typed several sentences then deleted them. He took out a voice recorder and listened back to a string of characters and short bios, sighed, and set it down.

4:40 p.m.

He forgot to turn on autosave, losing an hour of work in the process and slammed down the laptop lid.

8:50 p.m.

He scratched out several passages he'd written down in the notebook, then cracked open a beer and headed outside for a cigarette. He spotted a large coffee can full of cigarette butts on the deck.

Lung cancer. Right.

10:00 p.m.

"Damn."

Collin exhaled and looked at his watch, defeated, exhausted, and in disbelief. With all his boyish fantasies and daydreams about

Bramwell's Magic Cabin, the promise of his hands flurried in ease of words, Collin had come up empty.

He took a long drag at his station next to the overflowing coffee can. He closed his eyes and savored it. *Let it come,* he thought. *Let it come.*

A rustle in the woods opened his eyes. It came from several places around the cabin, but at the same time, further away. Collin couldn't tell.

"Hello?"

The hollow sound reverberated off every surface of the cabin exterior. Collin immediately regretted it. He turned, taking stock of all the lights on in the cabin. The rustle continued, louder, from more places. *The wind, maybe?* No draft at all, no reason for it.

Collin took two short and panicked drags and headed inside, locking the three locks behind him. He snatched his keys, phone, cigarettes, and laptop and sidled to the back room.

Stephen might have had the thought of quiet movie nights with Andrea back here, while the girls giggled upstairs until they fell asleep.

Upstairs.

Collin hadn't even checked there. He hit the light switch at the bottom of the stairs, light-footed to the front door light panel and switched off the ground floor lights. He tiptoed quickly to the stairs and ascended.

Just animals.

At the top of the stairs, Collin took stock of the dark below. He chose the larger of the two bedrooms and plopped down on the bed with his arms full of hodge-podge. The rustling was still out there yet seeming faint at this altitude. The window of the bedroom looked out at the front of the cabin. Thick heavy blackness. He checked his phone. No missed calls. Not even from Jim. Strange. Fourteen percent battery. He shot upright.

"The chargers. Shit."

Collin gingerly descended the stairs in the dark and fumbled around for the last known location of his laptop and phone chargers. *Bingo.* By the desk in the corner. His eyes still fluttered for vision and caused him to overshoot the location of the metal umbrella bucket. It crashed to the floor, ceasing the outside rustling. Collin stood quietly for a few moments. He stepped slowly towards the chargers and grabbed them from the wall, constantly blinking. He finally found the stairs.

KNOCK, KNOCK

Collin gasped and threw his hand over his mouth to stifle the sound and took to the stairs.

"Please don't creak. Please don't creak," he whispered. His breath was shallow and quick. One step up, two steps, no creaking.

KNOCK, KNOCK

"Shit!" He galloped up the remaining stairs, ducked back into the bedroom and waited. And waited.

It had been an hour since the last knock. Then two. Then three. Three percent battery. He'd forgotten to charge it. He fumbled for the outlet behind the nightstand, and plugged it in. He fell onto the bed, fully clothed, and let sleep take him. A low hum in staccato beats melded with chirping birds. Collin slowly rolled to his side. His phone was lit up. Erin.

"Hello?" Collin groggily whispered.

"You haven't even looked at the separation papers yet, have you? I'd like you to sign off this week so I can get things moving."

"Erin, honestly, what time is it?"

"It's 10 a.m., Collin. Rise and shine. Why haven't you looked at the papers yet?"

"Because I'm still processing it all, Erin. And we've got six months. You'll forgive me if I want a little playback before I sign my life away."

"Your life? Are you shitting me? *Your* life, Collin? My life has been housekeeper while you drive yourself nuts trying to be Number One Author."

"It's provided really fucking well for us though, hasn't it? Really fucking well."

"I would provide better if we weren't funding all your sister's rehab stints!"

"Erin, leave Kate out of this."

"Oh, I wouldn't dream of hurting your nutso sister, Collin, wouldn't want another meltdown."

Collin could feel the heat in his face rise and his teeth grit. California was the "half-state," and he knew he'd need to keep it reined in to keep her satisfied at 30 percent.

"Oh, I know, Erin, you don't have any dreams."

"I had dreams Collin!"

"No, you didn't, Erin. You quit acting the minute we met. You wanted a three thousand square foot house in a sunshine state and two kids and a country club membership, and you got it."

"I wanted to paint!" Erin was breathless.

"Since when? And why didn't you?"

"Fuck you, Collin. Look at those papers!"

Silence.

Collin shuffled to a stand and placed the phone in his pocket. He headed to the en-suite bathroom for a leak and ran the water. A brown clunk. "Fuck it."

Collin pulled the laptop and chargers to his chest, tucked his cigarettes into his shirt and headed downstairs. At the sight of the tipped-over umbrella bucket, he remembered the rustling.

The sun was bright, the air calm. Opening the door, the woods looked alive. Birds flitting, a deer running. All was right. Collin brushed away any fear of the previous night. Woodland rumblings. The usual nighttime animal banter was all. He stepped out onto the front porch and lit a cigarette, taking a nice long drag while leaning against the front door. His head rife with ideas.

Maybe that's what Bramwell was getting at. Letting it come.

Collin noticed something that wasn't on the deck before: a small brown package.

KNOCK, KNOCK

"Fuck!"

A disembodied knock, against nothing.

"Nope!" Collin shrieked, dropping the cigarette on his foot, ashes down.

"Gah, Christ!"

Collin reared back and kicked the package off the porch. He rushed into the cabin and slammed the door behind him. Panting, he stood with his back to the door.

KNOCK, KNOCK

"Leave me alone!" Collin was frantic.

KNOCK, KNOCK

Collin flung open the door.

"This is a private residence!"

The package lay planted in its original place. Collin approached it cautiously and lifted it. He looked around sheepishly and, against better judgement, brought it inside.

Collin stared at the package on the counter, then approached it, putting his ear to it.

"No bomb." He rubbed his face at the idiocy of it all.

Never taking his eyes off the box, he grabbed a steak knife and sliced the top. He winced and, with one eye open, spread the top wide. A small, plastic, jade-colored bracelet with a glass stone in the center. An intense wonder in his eyes turned to fear. The bracelet was eerily familiar and the bile in his throat grew. He closed his eyes and swallowed hard. Whether Collin Auberon wanted it this way or not, he was about to let it come.

The sticky scent of soda-streaked floors, Love's Baby Soft and stale Michelob breath clung in his nostrils. Collin stood, eyes closed, knife in one hand, bracelet in the other, like a conduit. His expression was soft, bemused. Collin was lost and fine with it. And just like that, he was found.

Chapter Six: Loser

A cheap "Class of '87" banner hung disjointedly over the gymnasium door. Bowie's "Let's Dance" blared over the speakers. The dance floor was a sea of bubble-shouldered taffeta and stiff hairstyles. A tall vision in a seafoam green dress made her way across the floor to a feathered-haired Collin Auberon in a white tuxedo.

Heather Jeffries, a husky-voiced, levelheaded senior at John Adams Senior High School, was bored. "Hey loser."

Collin fumbled with his suit pants that were becoming increasingly tight.

"You look good, Heather." Collin glanced at her and searched desperately for another point to stare at. Heather lunged for a hug. Collin took a deep inhale of her, keeping his hand on her side.

"You wanna get out of here? Carrie's got a few six-packs in her trunk. Her parents are out of town, you could stay."

"Come on, now." Collin pushed her off.

Heather rolled her eyes and let go of Collin. "Here we go." She crossed her arm in a huff.

"What?" Collin took stock of her. Her freckles. How she was wearing the hell out of that dress. How the lights shot blue and pink through her strawberry hair. How he wanted her.

"Kiss me, right here, right now," she said.

"No way! Isn't your date Gorilla the Hun?"

"Greg Hunter is all bark."

Collin stood back, stunned. "Yeah, tell that to Jerry Kale's face last week. You're out of your mind." Collin shrunk against the wall.

Heather moved in to kiss him. He softened and held her tight. A sharp shock of pressure between his shoulder blades sunk Collin; he was breathless. A tall, young blonde man, bulging out of his tuxedo at the neck, stood over Collin who'd hit the floor and didn't notice. Greg Hunter had arrived.

"The fuck is going on here?" Greg shouted and cracked his bulbous knuckles.

"Greg!"

"You shut up, Heather!" Greg grabbed Collin by his lapels and lifted him. "I'm rearranging this guy's face!"

"Hey come on, man!" Collin managed to squeak out.

"Leave him alone, Greg!"

Greg tossed Collin against the wall. "You know what? I got a better idea. Meet me outside, at ten o'clock tomorrow, by the marina. We'll see who's top dog."

The small crowd that formed found other things to look at and Greg grabbed Heather's wrist and pulled. She leaned back in to Collin. "Come and get me in three minutes, parking lot, we'll make a break for it."

Seafoam was swallowed in the movement of dancing bodies but was spotted near the rear gym doors. Collin raced to follow and was interrupted by a tear-stained, disheveled Katie Auberon.

"Stop, you sonofabitch!" Katie pushed him.

"What the hell!" Collin's eyes were transfixed on Heather's, her smirking back at him.

"Stop! Stop! We have to talk about Steve. Can we go outside, somewhere quiet please."

Collin rolled his eyes and pulled Katie to the side, grasping both shoulders. "Katie, honestly, not right now."

"Collin! He touched me and he wouldn't stop, you need to listen to me!"

"I got you to be a date for the senior prom and now you're complaining?"

"Yes, Collin, a date, not a whore! Why would you set me up like this? He violated me!"

Heather looked at him across the gym, her brow furrowed in concern. Katie wailed as another small circle slowly formed around Collin.

"You wanna ruin the rest of my fucking high school life, Katie? Keep going!"

Collin's forehead stuck to Katie's in embarrassment. "Katie, seriously not now! Do you know how many freshman girls would kill to go to prom with a senior?"

Katie went limp in his hands, and she sobbed openly.

"Collin, he wouldn't stop!" Her volume rose. She yanked Collin by the lapels and began to bawl loudly. Collin tried to dislodge her fingers from his suit. The crowd grew large.

"Hey Auberon! Maybe don't bring your little sister to the prom!" Greg Hunter hollered from across the gym. Greg headed out the back doors with a more-than-pissed Heather.

"Dammit Katie, way to fuck up my night!" He finally broke free of her.

"I hate you! You fucking hear me? I hate you! You're a horrible brother!"

He took off out the back doors; Heather was nowhere to be found.

The parking lot was crowded with wilted corsages and beer cans. Collin walked down the parking lot to his friend Richie's car.

"Hey, I hear your sister really wailed Steve Mexin in the nuts." Richie handed him a beer.

"Perfect. He'll be wanting to kick my ass next."

Richie popped open his beer. "Oh yeah? Who's first?"

Greg bellowed behind him from his car. "Look out dumbass, fucking geek!" Greg tossed a half empty beer can at him, soaking his whole left side.

Heather left her friend Carrie to head to Greg's car alone as she sidled up next to Collin. "Come on!" she whispered. "Take me with you, let's go somewhere."

Collin glanced sideways at Greg talking loudly out of his car window and chugging beers with three other meatheads.

"Heather, I don't feel good about this."

"About me and you?" She seemed breathless, waiting for his reply.

"About my lifespan after this."

"Come on, Collin. Your cheap little Vega is all I need."

A mess in pink taffeta came meandering down the parking lot to hoots and snickers. Katie picked up speed as she saw Collin. Collin grabbed his head, frustrated.

"Fuck, man. No!"

Katie raced to Collin and clung to him for balance. "Oh my God, Collin, thank God. Please can we go?"

Greg began to honk furiously. "Heather! Get the hell in the car!"

Heather paid no mind and turned her attention to Katie. "Oh my God, Katie, are you alright?"

"She's fine!" Collin snapped. "Katie, go with Danielle and them, come on, I gotta take Heather home."

"Are you fucking serious right now, Collin?"

"Yes, I'm serious, Katie! Jesus Christ, the both of you!"

Heather is taken aback. "What the hell did I do?"

"You don't really like me, you just wanna get away from him." He pointed to Katie. "And now I gotta take your sorry ass home because you can't act like a grown up."

Greg punched his horn and roared for Heather, the two dins almost blending. Heather and Collin stared at each other in a tense silence. He motioned for her to leave.

"Goodnight, Katie." Heather brushed Katie's shoulder and Katie gave a shy smile. Heather slid into Greg's passenger side.

"Fuck! Finally." Greg leaned over Heather and pointed at Collin. "See you tomorrow, dick wad!"

Greg's car peeled out of the parking lot, reaching sixty before it hit the road on two wheels, narrowly missing an oncoming car. The car pitched over the marina embankment to the pathway below. A flurry of teens rushed across the street, blocking traffic, some tumbled their way down the sides of the embankment, some skidded, some watched from the road. Collin headed the pack of skidders. The car smoldered, roof side down, too short to make sense. A mangle of limbs sat within the tin trap. Heather, thrown from the car, was face down, her body twisted and broken like a dropped doll. Collin couldn't help but be frozen in terror. Minutes passed, the crowd grew then disappeared as quickly as it came. The glass of Heather's bracelet reflected in the ambulance lights.

A giant gasp and series of labored inhales and exhales broke the conduit of woeful memory. Collin's mind was back in the cabin and awash with anguish. He dropped the bracelet and knife like hot potatoes and backed away, ashen. He had locked that memory away with so many others. The bile rose in his throat again. A husky voice broke the silence.

"Knock, knock."

Collin screamed. Jagged fingernails tapped the counter, leaving maroon circles behind. He slowly followed the fingers to the wrists and hands as they gathered blood-soaked hair and moved it to one mangled shoulder.

"Heather?"

"Hey loser."

Collin swiftly passed out.

The kitchen was dim, Collin blinked and shot his hands up in defense. His skin was cold and damp. He slid up the wall slowly, taking stock of the entire ground floor. No box, no bracelet, no knife.

He checked the silverware drawer and counted the knives. Six. Six of everything.

"Fuck." He felt wired, blanched, and bloated. He inhaled sharply and reached for his cigarettes. He'd really need to think about quitting these things. He shakily lit one and took a deep drag. His eye was drawn to smudges on the counter. Upon closer inspection, dark maroon with small swirls. He lurched back.

"Still here." Heather giggled. Collin screamed, dropping the cigarette out of his mouth. He scrambled for it.

"What do you want?" He closed his eyes tightly, slowly opening one.

"What do *I* want?"

Collin backed up. Heather's naked foot stepped directly on the lit cigarette.

"Heather, please, please don't kill me!"

Heather stopped. Her neck was broken and the right side of her face, a road-rashed mess.

"I'm not going to kill you, you moron." She sighed. "I want you to remember."

Collin was blubbering and trying to steady himself.

"I do! I do, I'm so sorry. I put it all away, it was just too much." Heather turned and walked towards the large oak desk at the edge of the room.

"Sit. There."

"Why?"

"While it's still fresh. Tell them about me."

"No! Heather, I won't. Those memories are mine."

"Tell them!" Heather leaped at him in an instant and sat heavily atop his chest. Thick brown liquid from a hole where her eye should be trickled into Collin's mouth.

"Okay. Okay, I will." He closed his eyes and stood. Heather, back by the desk, gently pulled back the desk chair.

Collin sat at the laptop, obedient but shaken. He stared at her, as she faced away from him, her one good eye taking in the cabin. The profile of the young, gorgeous girl he'd spent over a decade of his first eighteen years deeply yet quietly loving.

"Okay?" Collin said meekly.

She turned to face back at him. "Start from the beginning."

"Heather, why?"

"To write your wrongs, like the man said."

Collin thought back to Stephen Bramwell. Back to the pain and tension in his eyes, and the look of utter relief as they made their handshake trade of the cabin.

"You sorry sonofabitch, Stephen. I wonder who came for you." Collin said quietly. He turned back to Heather. "My wrongs?"

"You knew what you should have done. You knew you had all the time in the world to sneak away with me and waited. You didn't have the balls and blamed it on everyone else. I could've been yours, instead of …" Heather outstretched her broken limbs. "You blamed Katie after that. All she needed was you, Collin. For you to listen. She was never the same."

"I know, but if it wasn't for her … It was all too hard to manage."

"What? You would've come after me if you had the gusto? No. You were afraid. Just like you've always been afraid. And you blame it on someone else. It's always 'if you didn't, I wouldn't have!' Poor Collin, the world's taken so much from you, it's so hard. But you don't think about how much you take from them. Isn't it getting a little old, Collin?"

Collin swallowed hard and his lips parted. The anger was there, but the counterargument plainly absent. Heather stood at the edge of the desk, breathing heavily in his ear. "Now. Write. Don't stop until I say so."

Collin clicked away mercilessly while Heather paced the ground floor of the cabin. Every now and then, he caught glimpses of her. She bounced about the cabin on twisted limbs, leaving maroon shapes on the floor. The sun disappeared below the tree line and Heather stopped bouncing. Collin looked up at her hands on the edge of the desk. He sat back, his eyes red and pleading. She came around behind him and placed a hand on his shoulder. He instinctively clutched it and nervously pulled away.

She smiled. "There."

"I'm so sorry, Heather."

"I know."

"Are you okay with me changing your name? No one will know."

She stared at the page, reading nothing, just shining in the laptop light. "I'll know, that's all I needed. Don't read it again until you leave. Promise me. It'll be perfect."

"How did you find me?"

"Oh, I've been waiting for quite a while, I knew you'd get here eventually. Who do you think told Stephen you'd make a good option for the keys to the kingdom?" Heather gestured around the cabin.

"Let it come," he whispered. "Shit." Collin closed his eyes and could feel her walk steadily away from him.

"There will be others. And they will not be as nice. Or as patient. Or as beautiful."

Heather twirled, making Collin laugh. He took in the view of her in a few moments longer and watched in horror and amazement as she slowly healed, forming the face of the girl he remembered. He began to cry.

"You should get some sleep," Heather said.

"Can you stay?" He shook his head furiously at the notion. Who was he to ask such things? Of a girl? Of a ghost? He put his face in his hands. "Heather."

She was gone. Alone again. He titled it "Jade" and clicked save.

He walked over to the counter to grab a cigarette and checked the box—only three left. Taking quick notice of the pristine kitchen counter, devoid of maroon swirls. "Who came for you, Stephen? Who or what the hell came for you?"

Collin finished the last of this pack in silence. He ascended the stairs with melancholy pushing him forward. He was numb and feeling everything at once.

What was this place? Was it real? Was it anything more than a prison madhouse?

KNOCK, KNOCK.

Collin continued upstairs, unfazed. He slowly got undressed, listening to the knocks continue as he drifted off to sleep.

Collin was up early, expectant. He felt gritty, unwashed. He rolled his tongue over the film on his teeth and headed straight outside, reporting for duty. Boxes of assorted sizes awaited him. Collin scooped them all up in a thrust and brought them solemnly inside. He tackled the smallest first and broke the binding. A boy's shoe caked with mud. Instantly familiar. Collin broke down, anxiously wiping the tears out of his eyes. He grabbed the second and ripped it open. He removed a book, *Treasure Island.* Collin lurched. The last box was the heaviest. He took his time with it. A handgun. Nothing familiar at all. Never owned one, never shot one. He walked back to the front door and closed it slowly.

A tall thin boy caked in mud stood on the couch. His face was grossly disfigured and swollen on one side where a wound wept slowly and percolated. The boy's eyes widened, and his mouth opened in a scream only to pour water and clay mud onto the floor.

Collin choked.

"Hello Henry."

Collin laboriously headed to the desk and picked up the voice recorder. He flicked it on and breathed heavily for a moment, surveying the great room. Then he began.

"Henry Eddard. He wanted to fight me for stealing his idea for *Due: Private Detonation.* I told him to meet me at the far bank and we'd square off. He never made it, he fell into Capstan Bend River and drowned. Age fourteen."

Collin bawled and placed his hands on his knees. His eye caught the sensible shoes of a woman standing, chest crushed. Her soft smile, a cruel juxtaposition against her exposed ribs. The woman began to speak, labored and bubbling. Nothing of use. Collin's legs gave out, sending him slumping against the desk. He continued into the voice recorder.

"Florence Callum, a friend of my mother's. I stole the copy of *Treasure Island* she used to prop up the heavy china cabinet that eventually fell and killed her. Age thirty-four, I think."

He clicked off the recorder. His tears blinded and choked him. He stared at the ceiling and turned away from the woman and boy.

You don't realize what you're taking from them.

"God forgive me." He stared at the revolver for a beat then pushed the recorder back on.

"A handgun. I—I don't know what this is."

A voice behind him spoke. "Of course you don't. You're a horrible brother."

Collin's guttural scream cut through the quiet wood. He leaped out to the back room in a raging sob, clinging to the back window, only to catch sight of thousands of cardboard boxes that stretched like a winding stream through the forest.

How many times can you ignore being ignored? There are no surprises anymore. No living room dances, no brushes against me in the hopes of a tryst in the late hours. No flowers, no small glances of fire.

Nothing.

Just heat. Hot in my stomach. Hot enough to set fire to it all. To relieve him of the burden of loving me. It's just been so hard for him I guess. So hard to love me. Am I hard to love? Perhaps.

But I love him to death.

—Agnes Hardiman (Journal Entry, 2008)

THE LEFTOVER

Agnes Hardiman was sad. Knock-down, drag-out sad. She couldn't break herself out of the habit of making two cups of coffee. Of laying out socks and boxers on the edge of the bed each morning. Sometimes she'd even turn the shower on while she started breakfast just to maintain the familiarity. *She'd grow out of it*, she thought. For starters, Agnes had no memory of anything between the day Edgar died until arriving at the funeral. No rush. It would all come back in time. Yes, Agnes Hardiman was sad, indeed.

With a bang and a whimper, Edgar Hardiman had passed away shortly after having sex with his wife somewhere between the afterglow exhalation and what should have been the cuddle. After thirty-five years with Crossgate Financial, Agnes collected Edgar's belongings from the office. Pictures of the two of them, the dog that died seven years ago, some loose Viagra, a cut-out picture of the boat he wanted to retire on. A lifetime of plans made for the next chapter, like taking Agnes up to Boldt Castle on Heart Island for her 60th birthday.

She shook hands with the partners and the company president, accepted a tight hug from Edgar's assistant Melody, who seemed, to the trained eye, more overwrought than she should have been.

Lumbering into the house with a rolling suitcase in tow, full of Edgar's company wins, losses, and otherwise, the chime sound of the grandfather clock hit her square in the face. And Agnes would curse it, as she did several times a day. She tossed the suitcase inside the doorway, flipped the clock the bird and slammed the door.

The chime would only startle Agnes, not Edgar, who would keep on circling his Sunday crosswords or laughing under his breath at Beetle Bailey at the kitchen table. No shudder, no quick inhale. Just went on living. This wooden nemesis was Edgar's pride and joy. The clock was passed down from his mother, who always hated Agnes, and it stood like a disapproving crone on the edge of a living room filled with Princess House and JC Penney Home. It never seemed to *fit*. The wood color was too light or too dark for the other pieces in the room, too dated, too Mother Hardiman.

He used to fawn over lawn mowers or sports paraphernalia or cars, especially his red vintage Mustang with its smooth beige leather backseat where Edgar finally talked Agnes into letting him come in the back door. But for Edgar, this clock was his new showpiece and jaunts to the Mustang grew fewer and fewer until eventually, Edgar purchased a housing tarp and shoved it to the back of the garage.

Agnes burst into tears that gave way to a scream. She'd been doing that a lot lately, like a woman possessed, bouncing from emotion to emotion. Putting on lipstick for no reason, clipping outfits from magazines that Edgar would've looked good in, drawing incredibly hot baths in the afternoon, and smoking Edgar's cigarettes. She'd developed a taste for them now. Anything to chase away a feeling. Mostly that awful, nauseating feeling. A feeling that was back as strong as the first day she saw it.

A red thong peeking out from under their bed.

Agnes was a Hanes brief five-pack gal these days. Even when she wore French lace in the '80s, Edgar didn't like how it scratched him when they rolled around in bed, so this polyester ruffled dental floss should have turned him off completely. But there they were, bunched under a frame caster. A size small.

Agnes did the only logical thing she could think of at the time. She threw it in a paper lunch bag and drove it all the way to the Kroger's and dumped it in the dumpster. Edgar was incredibly attentive that week. A new coat, fancy dinner, and that sexy immersion blender she had seen at Bed Bath and Beyond. Also, something new: weekly cash to "buy herself something pretty."

Hush money.

Agnes was still completely crushed, heartbroken, and suspicious, but she'd learned a few things watching prime time soap operas. Never let them know you know. Her 'something pretty' went from a nice silk scarf or costume jewelry to specialty plants. She could see them now, out the kitchen window growing higher and higher.

Bing-bung!

Agnes cursed again and looked at her watch, perplexed, 2:37. The clock must be off, it rang only at twelve and five, as Edgar adjusted it to. Also, how long had she stood in this daydream?

Running the bathwater for her second over-115-degree bath of the week, Agnes stood, her naked reflection in the mirror. She stepped slowly in, her neck arching back, her body inching away from the heat. Sinking down, in the horizon of the tub edge with the sweet musk of the Calgon bubble bath heavy in her nostrils, Agnes remembered the second time. Magnolias. Faint but slowly insidious. It drove Agnes crazy that day, and she traced all over an empty house for the smell. Second floor bathroom hamper, Edgar's dress slacks—the crotch to be exact.

Agnes made barbecue chicken and corn that night, with mint juleps. While clipping roses for the table, a quick trim of the oleander leaf in her new garden would go virtually unnoticed. She wore her pink kitchen gloves and rolled it in with the mint on a piece of wax paper, put the wax paper in a Ziploc, inverted the gloves and threw them out with the knife stating it was bent. She wrapped *that* in a dish towel for safety and took the garbage out straight away. She decided on a Vodka Lemonade instead. Watching Edgar patiently for what seemed like days only resulted in Edgar throwing up violently for a few hours and passing out in his short robe on the recliner in the den.

Bing-bung!

A violent splash jolted Agnes back to the present and sent water out of the tub.

3:28.

That goddamned clock. Agnes lowered back into the water. The heat made her wince, but she was getting used to the shock.

The burn. It had taken the place of Agnes making small cuts on her outer thigh. Much less noticeable, more time spent. Agnes could let the scalding water cut her as long as it wanted, until it exhausted itself. She fixated on the cheap white clock that spelled "Bath," its corny rounded letters with the wooden peonies that accented it. A gift from Edgar's mother. "Yard Sale Wins," she called them. Marilyn Hardiman would not spend more than ten dollars on anything she "could make herself."

Agnes sank, eyes wide, to the bottom of the tub. She could see it clearly, Edgar toppling, the blood, her screaming, the service, the whispers. She could see it and hear it all.

Bing-bung!

Agnes shot up and gasped, a gulp of water caught in her throat. Choking, she pulled her body over the side of the clawfoot tub in the center of her personal bathroom—another hush gift—and fell onto the floor, heaving.

Bing-bung!

3:49.

Flinging on a robe, Agnes flew down the stairs, tripped but caught herself, staring at the very same step that cracked Edgar's skull in two. She steadied herself and walked timidly towards the clock. She lifted the hatch to open the clock wind, but it was caught on something. Even moving her fingernail over the edge to find a pry spot produced nothing. The sonofabitch had been glued shut. She had wound it the day before Edgar's untimely spill as it was inching towards 4:40. 12 and 5, only. That's the way Mother Hardiman liked it.

That was it, the way *she* liked it. Edgar had glued the hatch shut. Letting Mother have the last say through the clock. Even in death the woman was ruining her life. Rifling through the kitchen junk drawer, Agnes found it. The black and yellow Stanley hammer that swung too hard and was top heavy. A "fortunate factory mistake," Edgar called it. It was time to rid the house of Mother Hardiman.

Agnes had never smiled so hard than on the day Marilyn Hardiman died. Every meal tasted extravagant. The air was thick with perfume. She was brimming inside but the only solace she could muster for her husband was the occasional circular back rub. The broad reaching "there, there" condolence. She had never once seen a parent helicopter their child with such abandon. Especially not when that child was a middle-aged man of fifty-nine. At first it seemed jovial, kind even. But as the years went on, Agnes stood angrily by as Marilyn cut his meat at the table, tucked his napkin in his collar. Came over to help him floss. Dug through his laundry hamper for worn socks and underwear to prove that Agnes just liked seeing him unkempt. Yes, the sky was beautiful at high noon when they pronounced Marilyn dead. She may have even started humming to the flatline tone.

Bing-bung! Bing-bung!

Agnes twirled the hammer in her hand.

"So, you wanna play ball, you old witch? Do ya? Fine. Let's see how you like these apples."

The first swing sent Agnes's hand jolting. Not a scratch. The clock couldn't be more than fiberboard on the front yet took a beating like steel. The second swing hit the glass. No damage, no shards. She took to beating the clock repeatedly, from every direction, on every inch, until exhaustion.

Nothing.

Bing-bung!

Agnes dropped the hammer and started beating it with her hands. "You soul-sucking bitch! I hate you! Leave me alone!" She grabbed its side and pushed with all her might, sending it to the floor. Agnes's eyes darted around; she took a glimpse out of the picture window. A world undisturbed. No screams heard or reacted to. No clock startling the neighbors.

Silence.

Agnes tightened her robe and slipped on her sneakers lazily hanging by the front door, waiting for her to do something active. She entered the kitchen, flinging chairs left and right, creating a path and flung open the back door, running smack into a very alarmed Billy Woodruff.

"Oh gosh! Uh, hi Mrs. H, I was just wondering, um, with Mr. H gone and all if you'd like me to mow your lawn? No charge, of course."

"Billy, you're an angel! There is something I need. Can you help me move this clock?"

"Oh sure, looks heavy. You try to move it yourself?"

"As best I can!"

Billy took the larger base and Agnes the head. They moved quickly yet narrowly through the door. Agnes dropped her end, smashing the top off. Agnes smiled.

"Oh geez, Mrs. H, I'm sorry!"

"Not to worry, Billy, it's trash. Come help me get this to the fire pit."

With a heave, the grandfather clock smashed onto the stone pit amongst the wood and scrap branches Edgar had cleared a few weeks ago. A scream leapt out of Billy. Clutching his hand, a splinter about a half inch wide stuck out of his palm.

"Billy! My God, let me see!"

"I'm okay, Mrs. H, I'll have Mom get to it."

The grandfather clock squeaked as it leaned further into the pit. Billy took off home, pale as a ghost.

"The Pig Pit," Edgar called it. One day they were going to have that neighborhood pig roast. It ate up seven feet by four feet of their lawn. Couldn't agree on a pool, but Edgar got to have this monstrosity. It was worth it for her bathroom and, of course, for today. Agnes grabbed the lighter fluid and lighter that hung out in a bin four safe feet away from the grill and doused the clock. A weak chime came singing from it.

"Last words? Fine. Drown bitch." She clicked the candle lighter twice. No juice.

"No! Shit, come on!" Another click and its flame roared to life as she touched it to the ragged corner of the clock.

The clock burned for several minutes, scorching here and there. Never going to ash. Agnes took to finishing the last of Edgar's pack of cigarettes. Drag after drag, Agnes watched, her eyes never leaving the clock. The faux metal glaze on the pendulum faded and snapped, melting the plastic frame inside. Glass popped. Wood creaked. She exhaled slowly and let a small laugh leave her lips before she noticed something strange. The clock was repairing itself. The smoke seemed to travel inward instead of out. Creaks gave way to all out wooden moans, glass splintered, then fused itself back. Agnes watched in horror. The clock simply wouldn't die.

Agnes sprang back into the house and slammed the door behind her, panting and crying. Where could she go, who could she call, who would believe her? Mother Hardiman's constant insults regarding her taste in friends, most times to their faces, had driven them away. She hadn't worked since '94, no co-workers to confide in. Defeated, she walked through the living room and glanced up in horror. All the blood she had washed from the stairway was back. Agnes fell to her knees. Her eyes glazed over, she remembered.

She'd finally caught Edgar, this time in his office. She had gone to surprise him about a hot deal she had gotten for a cruise to the Bahamas. He was working late, and she figured he needed some cheering up. As she flung the door open, his secretary hopped off her knees and fearfully began to cry. Edgar sat there, naked from the waist down, fully erect and stunned. The secretary lurched and ran past a shaken Agnes.

Agnes bolted, dropping her Laguna for Two Cruise Line packet in the parking lot of Crossgate Financial. That night, Edgar arrived home in silence. Agnes sat at the kitchen table drinking bottle after bottle of wine. Edgar guzzled Jack Daniels and sobbed in his short robe. After tossing the bottle opener back in the utility drawer, she stared out into the blackness of the kitchen window. Her eyes danced for a moment, and she finally headed to bed, past a weeping Edgar.

Maybe it was the wine. Perhaps it was the emotional buzz and the fervent anger. On either account, at that moment Agnes was dead set on giving Edgar the most aggressively sexual night of his life. Skipping foreplay altogether, she all but pounced on him, though Edgar quickly took the lead. Hours later Agnes's eyes fixated on the ceiling in torment, Edgar in exhaustion. He got up to use the bathroom with a yawning stretch.

She watched him in the sliver of the door opening. In the mirror, Edgar made a small prideful smirk, and she tightened her grip on the "fortunate factory mistake" and twirled it unconsciously in her hands.

As he turned, she swung. He ducked, the hammer short of missing his head. Terrified, Edgar ran backwards. She swung again, in full cry now; she could barely see him but landed a blow square in the mouth, opening his jaw. Another blow to the head sent him down the staircase face-first, bounding down to the metal porcupine-shaped shoe scraper that took the rest of his face off. And there he'd lain, lifelessly, for twenty minutes as a naked Agnes meticulously washed the walls and the Stanley hammer. She guzzled what was left in the Jack bottle, put on Edgar's short robe, sat, sobbed, then called 911.

The blood was glaring at her again. She couldn't bear it, but there it was in all its glory, in all its shame.

Bing-bung!

Snapping out of her state and back into a post-Edgar perdition, she caught her ragged breath. The shadow of the clock loomed on the rug. But there was something strange about its shape this time. Wounded, larger. Agnes slowly turned and screamed. The putrid body of Marilyn stood over her, seething, and right beside her, a faceless lump in a navy suit.

Agnes sat there on her knees, choking the shock out of her system. Marilyn's mouth opened, releasing a foul liquid.

"Nobody hurts my baby and gets away with it!"

And with that, the grandfather clock teetered and fell sharply on a howling Agnes.

Silence.

Sloth

Provider. Family man. Veteran. Nice guy. Neighbor. Father. Husband. That guy that still announces he's home even after his wife died. Asshole. Shit stain. Jerk. Overbearing. Workaholic. Mean ol' guy. William.

Choose one. I'll answer to anything.

—William Stalk (7-Eleven Bathroom Stall Scribble, Springfield, CT, 20157)

DROP

"It's not going to be the same without you and Deb." Marjorie Peterson, childhood friend of William Stalk's wife Deb, neighbor, and all-around busybody fumbled with the box of curtains William had given her. "Life goes on, really, a house this size. Feels cavernous, especially now, with everything in storage."

William thought back to the giant lowboy from the dining room and how much of a bitch it was to get in the back of the moving van. And the sunken-in couch that he'd laid on for the last three months of Deb's life, all six foot three of him. He hated both of those pieces with a passion, mostly due to whacking his hip on the lowboy at least once a week, and the couch ceased to have a comfortable sitting or lying position without a spring up his ass. But to watch them go was more emotional than he'd imagined. The last pieces of Deb washing away in a yellow Penske truck.

"Yes, Marj, too big for just me and with you taking most of Deb's knick-knacks off my hands, a bit more spacious even then."

William's eyes narrowed. He was still bitter about her coming over, the day Deb passed, under the guise of consolation when all the while she was putting invisible stickers on everything of Deb's that she wanted. William ran his fingers across the top of the "SOLD" sign.

"It went fast. Deb kept such a beautiful and clean house I'm not surprised." Marjorie sheepishly tried to fill the silence.

"It did, Marj. Thank you for managing the reception, it was quite what she would've wanted. I appreciate that."

Marjorie waved him away. "And you so far away, I feel like I've lost both of you."

"Marj."

"I know, Billy, I'm sorry. But a little island in the middle of nowhere? *Old Man and the Sea.*"

Not even Deb had called him Billy, and he bristled instinctively at her familiarity. "Just feels right. My first love, the sea, 'til Miss Deborah Casper came along."

Old Man and the Sea indeed. The Naval Aviation Retirement Package was decent for two, and now even more manageable for one—and the brochure for the private rental of Keppel Island had looked inviting enough. No megawatt smile from a real estate agent on the cover, no hard bodied thirty-somethings frolicking on the sand with that pre-coital look in their eyes. Just a salt and pepper-haired man on a boat with beautiful greenery, seagulls, a sunset, and a quaint cottage behind him. Sold.

Marj kicked at the sidewalk. "Just be careful. Will you write to me, let me know how you're doing?"

William thought for a beat. He wanted to say, "No, I've got zero ties to you woman, get bent." But he didn't have the heart nor the energy. Leaving was the best thing. Nothing to come home to, and all the time in the world to forget.

"When I can. Be good to these new neighbors, no blind splitting, no cop calling, and no goddamn casseroles."

"Get on with you, old man." Marjorie shooed him off his own sidewalk to the curb. He gave a half hug and shook her hand.

Taking one last look at the house that Deb built, where they raised their only child, Jim, William felt like a stranger there. The last month was agonizing, and the place felt more like a hotel than a cozy home. The paint a lot yellower than he remembered, the front bushes severely manicured and cookie-cutter. Within sixty days, the Stalk home went from a tchotchke-filled hodge-podge of sentimentality to a cold beige-walled turn-key starter home. A tremble took William by surprise and with that, he hardily cleared his throat, entered his car, and headed for the hangar.

"Now she's a bit of a bitch if ya take off in the fog, eh?"

Provincial chatter pulled William out of his daydream. "Huh?"

"The plane's gotta warm up quite a bit on foggy or moist days. Make sure you account for gas."

"Of course, sure. Last maintenance?"

"Last Thursday. Tip top."

"Perfect, thank you." William's outstretched hand received a commanding yank.

"Tim Parns. As in Big Daddy Parns of Stonington."

William shook his head, embarrassed. "I'm not familiar, sorry."

Tim Parns bristled, and it was cut and dry from there. "Headed anywhere special?"

A wistful look caught William's face for the first time in half a year. "I'm he—"

A sharp buzzing in his breast coat pocket agitated him. The cellphone alarm to keep Deb's meds on time. *Deb Lung Medicine #1* in a pop-up label earned his gaze over Tim Parns.

Forty-seven days dead and he couldn't find it in him to delete them. William fumbled quickly with it, calming it for the time being.

"I'm heading to Keppel Island. Very excited."

Tim's eyes narrowed a bit as he removed his hat to scratch underneath. "No man is an island. You visiting or staying?"

"Visiting, but on a month-to-month agreement. We'll see how I like it." William managed a small chuckle, Tim did not.

Takeoff was a dream, smooth start up to a severe clear sky that became brighter and more gorgeous every moment that passed. Not a cloud or a care. Not entirely. Deb floated in and out of his mind. Odd inside jokes, troubles with Jim, arguments about another weekend spent alone. Burning several dinners while Deb attended her "book club" at the church rec room, later revealed to be Jim's AA meetings. The rise and fall of Deb's chest. Him, intently watching for it in the last days. The terrible morning of Deb's funeral hung in his vision like a haze in his peripheral.

He remembered staring ferally at the back of his son's head so hard he could have bored a hole clean through. Saying that they had a terse relationship was more than kind. It had been four years since

William had even laid eyes on Jim, forcing Deb to be gone half the day for Christmas Eves and Jim's birthdays. He couldn't bring himself to stomach him and now, as Deb laid in her casket in the Rose Suite of Feldman and Sons Funeral Home, Jim was all he had left of her, and he hated it.

Jameson Stalk—Jim to everyone outside of AA—only child to Deborah and William Stalk, and lifetime struggler with acute panic disorder, scanned the place for all exits out. Mapping the territory, he planned his small talk to stick to two key topics: the weather and condolence, "Terrible rain we've been having; it's a shame, yes, she was a lovely woman, thank you."

Jim ran his thumb along the silken weave of the casket lining. Ruffles, undulating seam patterns, gradients of pink and white. "It seems like more trouble than it's worth, doesn't it?" he said.

"A burial?" William snidely addressed his son, a son he hadn't looked in the face that day for more a than a second or two.

"A casket this grandiose, Dad. Mom wore the same robe around the house for the last twelve years."

"Well, I'll remember that when I bury you. No frills."

"Couldn't wait to get to that, could we, Dad?"

William walked over to the casket, eyes darting over the interior, then slammed it down hard, narrowly missing Jim's hand that was still caressing the lining.

"You don't deserve to see her. That nearly killed her—seeing you blue, comatose for weeks. All because some dumb broad left you. You're lucky she hung on another six years."

"It was more than Sheila, Dad. It was school, my job, the pills. And you know what the kicker was in all that? You told the doctor that if I'd have made something of myself and joined the Navy like you, at least I could've died in a war zone, not in some sanitary hotel that charges $500 for a bed pan."

"I'm sorry you were robbed of your valiant martyrdom over the town tramp. I haven't seen you shed half the tears for your mother as you did for that bitch. Your mother was never the same after that."

"No, she wasn't. She was worse."

"What do you mean, worse?"

"Mom had anxiety and depression for years, Dad."

"The hell she did!" William pushed Jim back away from the casket.

"Honestly, how can you be so oblivious? There were days you'd be off on some cross-country mission, and she would sit up watching TV until the morning news came on."

"So now she's a basket-case because she had insomnia?" William turned somberly, sighed, and placed her casket lid back up apologetically.

"She used to sit up all night with your 9mm."

In one swift beat, the lapels of Jim's jacket were near his neck and his shirt collar was seizing in on his throat. With his son pinned against the wall, it was as if time had stood still. The slow pulse of the vein above William's left eye, the sweat beginning to bead on his upper lip and the disjointed jaw shaping words he could no longer hear over the sound of blood pumping through his ears. And in an instant William released his grip on the jacket and Jim tumbled to the floor with a gasp, deaf to his father's words still rolling through the Rose Suite.

"You filthy sonofabitch! Lying bastard! I wish it were you, do you hear me? I wish it were *you*!"

Jim gasped and clawed the wall to right himself. The parlor assistant went unnoticed and quickly exited. "5-7-16-32-4." Jim coughed, finally catching some semblance of breath.

He stood, hands clutched to the wall as if in the hope that it didn't give way. "5-7-16-32-4. The combination to the safe. She'd have me get it out if her hands were shaking too much. At first, I thought it was for protection, ya know? You were gone for days at a time, just her and a young kid in the house. But one night I came down to sneak some twinkies she forgot to put on top of the fridge. She was spinning the cylinder, shoving it back into place. She put it to her temple and then would stop. And cry. She did it over and over. Every night you were gone."

William found a chair and sat, dazed. "Why didn't you tell me?" William looked at his son in sorrow. He examined the lines in Jim's face. He'd gotten older. Grey appeared on the side of his head, making the redness of his ears stand out.

"She made me promise, she told me you'd be angry with her if you found out."

"I've never been angry at her a day in my life."

"She was just sick, Dad. Trying to keep it together. We talked so much more after that. I made sure we did a lot together, kept her laughing." Jim cleared his throat a bit more.

William stood slowly, his face reddening. He couldn't settle on what to say exactly. He was angry for the time he lost with Deb, he was angry at Jim for giving Deb the angina attack that lead to the testing that revealed her cancer diagnosis. He wanted to blame Jim for lying, but he didn't have the basis as much as he had the balls. And now there was no time. He could hear the murmurs of mourners arriving in the entrance.

In a slow cadence, Jim made his way over to his mother's casket. He smoothed out the lining once more with the precision of a concert pianist tidying his station before a performance.

He gently whispered to her and kissed her forehead, and rose to a full stand, taking her in one last time.

"Jim." William inched closer.

Jim wandered towards the back of the viewing room. "She was a lovely woman, thank you." He took back his hat that had stood watch on the last chair rail. "I hope you've got an umbrella, terrible rain we're having today." He placed the hat on his head and exited.

One more pat on the back. One more handshake. Finally, time alone with her at last. William had been waiting to say everything. The private things. Nothing. Nothing came. Deb had been the most beautiful woman he'd ever seen, and now he didn't even know who he was looking at. The soft chubbiness of her round face faded into the hard ridges of her now sunken cheeks. The rouge and lipstick, the wrong shade. Her hair too tightly curled and parted on the wrong side. Five days ago, she was back, asleep, but back.

He swooned, bending on the casket with his full body weight, making it lean.

"Oh God, shit!" Staggering, the black spots took over him and the cold clamminess of his hand swiped him off Deb's casket, and tossed his head into the side, knocking him out. Now, it was just the two of them sleeping. Separately, like it had been for months.

A loud buzz and a pull in the pit of his stomach snapped him out of the Rose Suite into the plane in a steep drop. William quickly dropped the power and yanked on the control column.

"Fuck! Fuck!" The nose slowly leveled out. William took a deep inhale and let the raucous sweat glide into his eyes for a while, he couldn't loosen the grip on the column, not yet. He made note to definitely check his shorts upon landing.

Landing the plane was easy enough and he slowly taxied it into the three-sided hangar on Keppel Island. Odd-shaped but sturdy, the structure slowly creaked in the breeze.

William yanked his two large suitcases from the plane and noisily made his way to the cabin. The casters caught themselves in the sand and gave life to snake-like tracks and divots, making William curse every few feet. Looking up, he dropped the two over-sized nuisances and rested his hands on his hips and smiled.

Although he'd never met the owners of the island—Caroline and Harold—in person, he'd swear they were old friends. The communication was top-notch and jovial. The keys were right where they said they'd be, deadbolt and doorknob unlocked, and he opened the coastal home of his dreams. The sweet, salty smell of the ocean mixed with the dusty waft of the diesel generator made his nose twitch. Not a speck of dust or sand on anything. Beautiful views and comfortable furniture. The upper level revealed a loft he assumed was the bedroom.

"Hell. This is alright."

William kicked off his docksiders and opened one suitcase. He pulled out a small cool-pack thermal bag comprised of two six packs of beer and a few containers of mussels in cocktail sauce. He pushed through a small, enclosed porch, settled onto the front steps and into beach life. Letting the cocktail sauce hang out in his mouth for a while, he savored the taste, never wanting to forget this day, this moment.

But he was. The bits of the morning shook apart like fallen puzzle pieces. Standing with Marj, Big Daddy Parns, whoever the hell that was. Should he have known? The holding pull on the yoke to keep the nose of the plane out of the water. William shook his head, he couldn't fully remember that either. One thing he did remember was to check his shorts. He stood quickly and pulled the front of his tummy-slimming shorts wide in front of him. A-Okay.

The day was lethargic, just the right temperature, the sound of the pounding waves, magical. For a while. His ears were buzzing, and he could hear his own exhalations. He felt like an old fat bastard. He pondered Tim Parns' question. Visiting or staying? Truth was he was lonely as all hell already and the sun had only just begun to set. Four hours on this island of dreams already felt like the beginning of a nightmare. And he was getting sleepy. Mussels always made him sleepy. He'd forgotten that too.

He steadily packed away what he'd brought, mostly cans, a completely impractical lemon meringue pie Marj sent him off with, and a sack of oranges. Per the brochure, a food vessel stopped once a week, so he figured he could stretch the Chef Boyardee enough.

The coastal home was gorgeous, stark white with shaker furniture. Deb would've loved it, she always wanted a home that looked "just like a Southern front porch."

While staring down at an ornate hot pink sign on the kitchen counter that read, *"PLEASE ENJOY OUR VIDEO LIBRARY!"* it quickly occurred to William that he hadn't even truly explored the rest of the beach house.

William walked through the great room, with its *House Beautiful*-styled conversation corner, and parlor seating that sat perpendicular to the fireplace. A gold bar cart filled with your island alcoholic basics. A contact radio setup sat under a plastic dust cover on a spare table. In the corner of the grand room off the kitchen, lay a walk-in closet of sorts. Bookcases upon bookcases of DVDs, everything labeled with expert efficiency. Comedy, Rom-Com, Dark Comedy, Sci Fi Comedy, Sex Comedy. Nothing of interest here, too guilty to laugh. The Lime Green "TV" sign caught his eye. Everything from 1950s to now. *Laurel and Hardy*. Jackpot. DVD *Laurel and Hardy*, even better.

"Bingo!" He supposed he did want to laugh a little. As he headed back in to the kitchen area, he was caught by a faint line of orange haze that hung low along the horizon line. Dusk had officially arrived, and he figured it was best to get the rest of his things upstairs. Truly settle in. He lugged his two suitcases upstairs to the loft where a four-poster canopy bed sat amongst an exorbitant amount of seashell motif.

"Jesus that's ugly." He shrugged and tossed one suitcase to the corner of the room. He opened the smaller of the two, pulled out his shaving bag and headed to the ensuite bathroom. A basic all-white factory original with a hexagonal window that looked out at the hangar. The hangar looked ominous in this low light, like the whale that ate Jonah. He pushed his face against the window, catching something rustling along in the tall grass near the hangar wall. "What the hell?"

He jumped back, quickly switching off the bathroom light to head back downstairs to lock it up tight for the night. He found it strange to have a rod lock at the back door.

Perhaps to deter errant wildlife with opposable thumbs. William nervously cackled at the idea and pushed it closed quickly.

A lovely low breeze from the cracked-open kitchen windows swirled the curtains in a lazy dance. The air seemed perfect. Too perfect, and it made him think about the thing in the tall grass. He rolled his eyes at the thought and continued his trek to the refrigerator for a beer. In the corner of his eye, he noticed the horizon line shift. Then he saw something surface. A much larger splash than a sea bass would make. And he swore he'd seen feet. The water went still. He wasn't alone.

The brochure would've said. It would've warned. He shook his head almost violently as his mind raced through the horrible possibilities. Maybe that's what the locks were for. Maybe someone that was here never left like they said they were going to. The supply vessel wasn't coming until the end of the week, so no one would know he was missing until then, should it have gotten to him.

The shock of adrenalized panic turned his stomach and the faint taste of mussels danced in the back of his throat. He sat by the kitchen window for over an hour, staring at the section of water where he'd seen the feet. The occasional bass would leap and so would his heart, but nothing noteworthy.

He glanced at the clock in the great room. 9:30 p.m.

"Shit." William should've had a few beers in him already, outstretched, and cozy upstairs enjoying two side-splitting hours of *Laurel and Hardy*. He decided to end his patrol. Deliberate in the order of closest to the furthest from the front door, he switched off the downstairs lights.

He grabbed another two beers, shoved the DVD in his mouth and hightailed it to the loft.

The bed was incredibly comfortable and seemed to mold to him. After sleeping on the couch for the last three months of Deb's life, and the three weeks after it was over, it was nice to sleep outstretched.

He let out a yawn and wiggled his toes and hit "play all" on the DVD player's remote.

For hours he tossed comfortably, rolling over, coiling himself into the luxurious duvet. He had gotten back to the home screen and "Dance of the Cuckoos" played over and over. A drone took over the air. Right next to his ear.

Breathing. Labored breathing and a gasp and then, silence. William shot up screaming. His phone angrily buzzed against the lamp.

Deb Heart Med #2 8:00 a.m. That's all it was. Just the phone. But the gasp. The gasp was something else entirely.

He looked up at the ceiling, his eyes a fervent flutter desperately trying to adjust. Dark green smears between the grooves of the clapboard ceiling. Mold. He hadn't noticed it in the low light of the night before and it couldn't have mattered less, he was dog-tired.

William let the shower spurt for a few minutes before it finally ran clear. It was lukewarm at best, but he stood, face in the water, counting his breaths.

I don't know what's going on, Deb. I think … I think I'm losing it. I miss you. I miss everything about you. And I'm seeing things, I'm just … just so tired.

William stepped downstairs to a bright great room. The shower hadn't helped, only cleansed. He'd hoped it would wash away the tension, the loneliness. The ick he still felt in his stomach from his argument with Jim three weeks ago.

Just call the kid. Dammit.

He pulled out his cellphone. Dead. No matter anyway, he couldn't even remember where he packed the charger and didn't imagine there was even service on the island. He stepped into his docksiders and walked out the front door.

A navy-blue dinghy writhed against its post and mingled in the tide fifty yards from the beach house. William pillaged the tackle shed and rowed about 100 yards from the shore line and dropped anchor and his line. The sun blazed on his back, and he couldn't decide whether he liked it or not. He'd hoped for some sort of relaxation or at least a day without a sense of missing something. He'd been errant since Deb passed. No longer needed to stand watch or remember treatments. Deb wanted to die at home and without a Deb, he felt worthless, and he knew each day on Keppel Island would only get worse. And with only one full day into his paid thirty-day jaunt, he would need a lot more beer.

Something in the water made the line dance.

"Come to Papa you chubby bastard, I've seen you's." He grabbed the line and it yanked hard, holding steady he pulled back and back, reeling as fast as he could. A bass flung out of the water, and knocked into the dinghy, shy of sending William overboard.

"Ha! I gotchu! Wooooo!" He pulled the hook out of the bass's mouth and held it to the bottom of the boat to minimize flopping.

It let out a few sick wiggles and stopped. "Perfect! You'll be a good haul for tonight." William launched forward. Something knocked hard under the boat. He steadied himself, grabbed the oars, and pitched the dinghy into gear. It was wide, whatever it was, and made smooth ripples in the water.

Faster.

It's back humped out of the water. Grey. Spinal.

Faster.

The boat rocked hard to the side, letting water spill in. William shouted out in panic. A shriek—he could hardly believe it was his.

Faster.

It bounded and dove swiftly and at the tail end … feet. This was no fish, crocodile, or shark. This was a man. A tall man at that.

Faster.

William chucked forward, running aground on the shore. He scanned the shore line, panicked. Nothing. Just the quiet, rolling tide. William grabbed the bass and sprinted to the beach house.

He tossed the fish in the sink and plopped down on the couch. His hands shook and his eyes burned an achy heat, dry from never blinking since the shoreline. He had soaked through his shirt and his heart was pounding in his ears.

"Fuck this, I need a drink." William headed for the bar cart. As he turned, he noticed a shadow take over the front porch.

A hum took over his head. He grasped it tightly and fell to his knees.

Let me in. Please, let me in.

"No! Get out of here, you don't belong here! Get away!" William pedaled back towards the back corner of the room.

Please, I've been looking for you. Let. Me. In.

With a shout and a drop, William passed out cold.

It was dark when William woke with a gasp on the cool floor of the beach house. He rolled over on his side and sobbed. It had all been for naught, his stay here. He'd tried to escape all the anger and the resentment and the love and all he'd done, in two short days, was lose his mind.

"Deb I can't do this alone! Deb!" he shouted into an empty home. He grunted angrily as his back protested from getting up off the floor to a stand. His eyes widened and he darted to the curtained front door and stopped short. The walls, the cracks, the windowsills, all bore a dark green slither from them. A root-like pattern of mold hung broad across the loft wall. He stood bewildered. Had he truly not noticed this before? Was he so happy to be here that warts and all he'd been blind to the view?

He locked the front door and took stock of the lock on the back door, still engaged.

He switched on the lamp on the mantle, not caring whether or not it alerted whatever was out there. He'd given up.

He turned to the video library and flicked on the light. A turquoise placard read, "Horror." His fingers nimbly raised the spines. *Alien, The Abyss, Dusk 'til Dawn, The Exorcist, Swamp Thing.*

"Absolutely not."

He headed back to the lime green comedy shelves and grabbed *The Odd Couple* and headed to the loft. The waft of less-than-fresh fish hit him square in the face.

"Aw damn it!" Stomping to the kitchen, he grabbed the bass and tossed it in the freezer. He washed his hands and wiped them on his pants.

In his bare-chested and boxer-laden glory, William laughed heartily at what an absolute curmudgeon Oscar Madison could be. It reminded him a lot of himself and Deb. Him, rough around the edges, her, all marshmallow and flower fields. A faint green line drew slightly from right to left on the screen.

"Shit." William searched for the remote to skip and was alarmed by static, he flung himself into the headboard. The screen went black. He panted in the darkness.

"Hello?"

The screen pinged back on. Amber glow vision, like a seventies photograph. A woman's hands on a gun. A gangster moll surely.

Maybe it was cut with a Columbo *episode.*

"One, two, three," the woman said as she spun the gun cylinder and placed it to her temple.

A scream leapt out of William, and he crawled out of the bed onto the floor.

"No! Deb, no!" He banged on the television.

"One, two, three."

"Deb! God dammit! Please!"

"One, two, three." She put it to her temple again and pulled the trigger. Click. Nothing.

William sat frozen, eyes and mouth agape.

Deb laughed. "Ah, safety." She put the gun down and turned quickly to a small weak voice.

"Mom?"

"Oh Jesus, no." William sobbed uncontrollably on his knees, almost praying to the television and watched helplessly as a young Jim hugged his mother tightly, her stroking and kissing his hair. Deb's gaze turned slowly to William, sending him reeling back.

"William?"

"Deb. I'm so sorry." He could only muster the words through deep inhales and whimpers.

"William?"

The television blared at peak volume and sent William recoiling and throwing apart the bed linens for the remote. A laugh track had swallowed Deb and Jim. William meandered about the bedroom before heading to the bathroom to vomit. Nothing but bile and dry heaves. He slowly exited the bathroom and turned off the light.

He was supposed to be angry with Jim. Furious even. That was the way. Deb was the good cop, struggling to understand how she could help her son. William was the bad cop, always with a piss and a moan. And as he thought back it wasn't just pain in her eyes when Jim was mentioned, it was guilt. Had she shown him that there could be a way out? It wasn't the poor kid's fault. He couldn't even dig up a bad word to say or think. Jim was clearly her rock when he was absent. Not the role a boy of nine needed to have. A solid chime rang out downstairs. Midnight, he presumed. He hadn't heard it last night—but as he'd seen, this house was full of surprises.

Limping and lost, he traveled downstairs to the open-plan area to the source of the sound. 12 a.m. The clock in the great room. The chimes rang out to "Sentimental Journey," and William's knees buckled, and he raced to a chair for stability.

Doris Day. Parker's Pickup Pub and Grille, 1964, Deb wore a yellow dress to their first solo date. A yellow one just like Doris Day's in *I'll See You in My Dreams* with Danny Thomas. Odd and out of place in a sea full of miniskirts and pigtails. But lovely.

"Dance with me."

Oh Deb.

He turned at a brush at his shoulder. A gruff scream leapt out of his mouth before he could catch it. There she stood, hair curled too tightly, and parted on the wrong side.

"Dance with me." Instinctively, he grabbed her at the waist and clasped her hand. He led, and as a self-professed "toe-stepper," she'd always liked that it kept her in step. They danced about the great room. Her smile was stiff and disjointed and William's eyes darted about her face for a semblance of life, of character. And it was making him ill. They bounded onto the front porch and down the steps, as if nothing were beneath them. Onto the beach they glided.

His gaze drifted sleepily to the cabin about twenty yards away. Somber and brown in the moonlight. Deb's makeup cracked around the corners of her mouth that never seemed to stop smiling, as if sewn that way. William pitched backward and she leaned in. He was exhausted.

How long had they been dancing? He could barely attempt another sway and his mouth, which hung open at the sight of his dead wife, was arid. A white pale figure moving in the water captured his gaze. The pounding of his heartbeat in his ears was back. The hum slowly trickled and on impulse he squeezed Deb tighter. He watched it intently until it caught him watching back. It swiveled in the water and dove deep. With arms. Two arms.

A man.

William let go of Deb and bolted towards the house and froze. The cabin was overgrown, rusty even, the steps littered with vines. The door hung ajar.

Beige fur house slippers shuffled along the beach, a pink terry cloth robe slapped gently about putrefying shins. Deb. Out of time. William, with so much time. Face to face again.

The perma-grin was gone. In its place, the rotting shell of the woman he fell in love with.

"Hi, William."

"Hello, love." William wept openly and pulled her in for an embrace. She smelled the same. Shalimar. Shalimar and sea … and rot. He pulled away quickly.

"You don't remember do you?" Deb's sad expression still coming through.

"That you've died? Of course I remember, I can't escape it."

"No. How you've gotten here."

"I flew." William said.

"Where is the hanger?"

William looked to the right. Empty and overgrown land where a giant hangar once stood. Not a trace of a frame.

"You lost altitude on the plane."

Deb was close behind him, he spun and teetered away.

"No! I—I got it back up! I got it back up and I've been here!"

"You were missing. The Coast Guard searched for you for a week. Fallen soldier."

"They didn't find me?" William circled in futility.

"Jim found you."

"How?"

A loud breaker crashes. The arms come back, gliding gracefully in the water. They make their way towards the shore.

"Easy. He was in the East River anyway."

"Deb." William understood that the wish he'd longed for— from the minute Deb passed—had been granted, and it was eating at him. Piece by piece.

"Well, he finally did something you asked him to do. He finally did it."

"No! Jim, kid? Jim?"

Deb turned her gaze to the sea and walked towards it.

"You never thought about him at all did you, William? He took care of me. Like a good son."

Out of the water, Jim stumbled clumsily ashore. His neck out of joint, ribs crushed and poking out from under a blue T-shirt. His sunken eyes hooked right into William.

"Now you have nothing but time. He wanted that for you. Every man is an island. Enjoy it, William."

Jim walked closely to Deb, who grabbed his face in her putrid hands.

"Mom?" Jim's pale grey skin glowed in the moonlight and Deb let go of his face slowly.

"Hello, Jim. Ready to go?"

Jim's pale corpse stared over at William. "I am taking her. She's mine. You don't deserve to see her."

William reluctantly nodded.

"Goodbye William, love."

"Deb."

Jim and Deb walked slowly into the sea, never attempting to swim, and disappeared within the tide. William sat on the beach, now knowing time is never ending, love is terminal, and the supply boat is never coming.

It's a shame, yes, he was a lovely man, how about this weather?

Gluttony

What is love without sacrifice? I love her. Every inch. Every sound. Every whimper and gasp. Everything that sparks the light in her eyes. Love, rich love. Down to the bone.

—Benjamin, A Sonnet to a Love Unknown, 1897

Maddalena

It'll be the death of you, young love, they always say.

She is the center of my universe and my reason for living. As if Mozart himself set the veins, sinew, muscle, and skin into full pulsing vitality graced with love and tenderness and that ruffian smile with a chip in her front tooth.

The white-hot electricity of our bodies as we further intertwined to and fro, in the clandestine alleyways near the river, hexed me with a new passion, Maddalena. I managed to scrape my way into affording Mrs. Benington's boarder house on the river for us. We drank until dawn to our nuptials, and I lay beside a sleeping love I'd never known.

Morning came and my eyes adjusted slowly to the glaze between awake and asleep, and to the round of Maddalena's hip and thigh, the small of her back, the nape of her neck and my arm bare to the bone and bloody in her mouth.

She had eaten me through and licked the bones clean as she worked her way upwards, tossing her head back to open her throat, taking more of me down to the gullet. I wiggled my bones to cradle her head and let love eat me alive.

Greed

It's not like I fell into it. I volunteered. If you volunteer, you're less likely to get asked. And I don't like being asked for much. Slink down, stay quiet, be quiet, get out. One. Two. Three. Four. Easy peasy.

I think of a square home in the middle of the desert, like one off of Architectural Digest or something. No real windows, just skylights, cameras to watch the place. All electric everything, little white cat or dog or something runnin' around.

That's what I think about. I'm saving up for all that. Hell, if you don't want time and a half, I'll take it.

—Eli Willis in conversation with Kev Fullerson, June 21, 2016

Things Are Tough All Over

Eli Willis's hair was far too thin to muster a full ponytail. State tollbooth operator's protocol said "nothing touching the collar" for men, but it seemed out of line to bug a nice fella like Eli about it, so there it sat flapping in the breeze off the back of his head like a plastic tube man. He was a waifish man with a quiet stare, too soft to cause any trouble. Amenable, good sense of humor, model employee.

"You gonna be alright here by yourself, scout?" Kev Harrison chided Eli.

Eli shook a stack of DVDs at Kev. "Got all I need."

"Porno?"

Eli looked quizzically at him.

"Yeah, right. Whatever. See ya later." Kev, on his way to celebrate his divorce, hopped in his lifted F-450 and did a quick donut in the dirt before taking off down the interstate.

Eli liked to take all the holiday shifts. Time and a half. Sweet, sweet music to most state employees. And today, Eli's solitary twelve-hour shift on the new east stretch of Route 57 on the Fourth of July 2017, was going to be a wild one. Route 57 was forty-seven miles between exits, which everyone agreed was the most idiotic and infrastructurally fucked way to go about it. But it brought the city new revenue, and restaurants popped up and along the route like a whack-a-mole. Five Guys, then a completely out-of-place Bed Bath & Beyond. Some hemp shops and crystal places, one tea shop, and one Sunoco. One. Idiotic.

Eli watched as the sky turned from blue to pink to navy, devoid of that mind-stream of consciousness man is supposed to get when alone amongst nature. A pants-less Kelly LeBrock pranced on the screen. He slowly spun the DVD case on the desk with his finger. A small rustle grabbed his attention. He stood slowly.

Coyotes.

Worse: headlights. Actual work.

He departed the plastic vertical partition and headed into the toll booth. A bronze eighties Mustang slowed down, popping the correct change in the bucket before zooming off, kicking dust in Eli's face. A few quick spits, and Eli watched it grow smaller in the distance with the wonder of a small child watching a plane head higher into the sky, then out of sight. As he headed back into the shelter, two shining and erratic beacons caught his eye. As they closed in, Eli noticed the slick bronze paint glistening in the low light, just like before. And there it was again, that eighties Mustang.

The man in the vehicle looked like he'd been roughed up a bit and struggled to reach his arm out of the window to place the change in the rusting metal bucket. Eli tipped his hat, and the driver sped off. Eli instinctively stepped back, avoiding the inevitable dust cloud. Even before the taillights were out of sight, he watched two more bright dancing lights careening his way. He unconsciously balanced on his toes, ready to dart in the opposite direction of the speeding car. He jumped right as the car sped through the toll—no money this time.

Over and over again, the car and driver seemed worse for wear than the time before: careening heavier, the lights brighter, more menacing, the driver bloodier, stupefied but hell-bent.

It was only this time that Eli spotted a bloody and disheveled woman in the backseat. The car arrived, jerking forward, left, then right. Finally, it stopped just past the toll shelter.

"Hey look, now, you in trouble, sir?" Eli shouted from behind the plastic vertical blinds. He grabbed the small pistol he kept taped under the counter, snuggled behind his videos, and eased the walkie talkie out of his pocket. A loud beep sprang the handset panel to life.

"Cresthill, do you copy? Looks like we got a Code 2 on Checkpoint 10 Hwy 57. Over."

Static.

"Cresthill? Dammit!"

On his way out of the shelter he closed the chute on the change bucket, locking the automatic arm mechanism. Eli came to stand in the driving lane behind the vehicle, locking eyes with the woman.

The driver squealed off with the woman banging a bloody hand on the rear windshield. Again. A puff of dust, red rear lights on his right, shining orbs of panic on his left. The bronze Mustang came to a screeching halt, inches from Eli. There was bile in his throat, rising, burning like well whiskey at a dive bar. He grasped the handle of the gun tight as he walked to the driver side and swallowed hard.

"Roll down your window, now!" Eli's pistol was low. The driver didn't move but looked at Eli in horror. He lifted his gun and pointed it at the driver. "Roll down your window, sir, now!"

The driver slowly rolled down the window. "You don't know what you're doin', man."

"Get outta the car or I'll shoot." His calm voice was a betrayal to the low rumble of vomit in the back of his throat.

"Look, Mister, just let me go. You're really making a big mistake here." The man's brow was a mix of blood, sweat and dirt, a light green glow from the dash within gave an ethereal hue to his dinginess.

Eli caught the eye of the woman in the backseat. His hand was surprisingly steady, a barrel pointed firmly at the head of the driver. "Ma'am, are you hurt?"

The woman surfaced, bloody faced. Eli stuck his hand in the window, placed the barrel on the man's head and unlocked the back door of the car.

"You're fucking crazy, man! You don't know what she's done!" The man wept and pounded the steering wheel.

"Where are you going with her?"

"Fucking nowhere at the moment! Please! Put the gun down. She'll kill us. You don't know what you're doing."

"Shut up! Ma'am, could you exit the vehicle, please?" Eli pulled the barrel off the driver's head and took two large steps backward, pulling a hard exhalation out of the driver. He pointed his gun back and forth between the two passengers.

The woman got out of the car slowly, and the driver gritted his teeth and pounded the dash in frustration. "She's going to kill us!"

Eli took a fleeting look at her forlorn face and let his eyes trace back to the driver.

"Ma'am, you go right around the back, now, through those panels, and sit. I've called this in, you just sit tight, okay."

Fuck you, Cresthill.

A whip of wind sent Eli stumbling back, slipping. The driver bounded out of the car, baseball bat in full swing, rolling it in his hands.

The woman screamed and ran to the back of the toll shelter. "Please stop! Help! Help! Oh God!"

"I'll shoot you!" Eli staggered back to his feet.

"I'd rather have *you* kill me, at least you won't tear me apart." The driver continued to swing. "You just made the biggest mistake, buddy. Now she's going to kill all of us!"

Eli kicked at the driver's chest and slipped.

The woman stood inside the shelter, just behind Eli. "He's lying!"

Eli was startled. "I said stay around the back!"

The woman ran to the back of the shelter, and hid behind a small desk, breathless and faint. The driver took a swing at Eli's ribs and connected. Eli raised the gun steadily before it was kicked free from his hands. The driver kicked Eli in the face, leaving him motionless half-in, half-out of the plastic partitions. The driver stepped over him.

"Come here, you little bitch. You can't hide from me. You wanna kill me? Come on!"

The woman reappeared from behind the small desk in the middle of the tiny room. "You don't know what you're doing! I wasn't going to harm you."

"You won't harm *me?* I just saw you destroy three people, and for what?"

"Please." The woman clung to the desk. Eli stood behind the driver and fired a shot into his head. The woman howled.

Eli didn't move to come closer. "You alright, ma'am?"

The woman nodded. "Yes, yes."

Eli didn't lower his gun. "You okay telling me why this man hurt you?"

"He thinks I'm a killer."

"Now why is that?" Eli was breathless, his grip on the gun holding steady.

"Because I am not like you, I have … abilities."

"One of them inhuman people?"

"We're very human, but yes. Enlightened." She walked forward. Eli backed up.

"I won't hurt you," she pleaded, "He was going to sell me. Every time I tried to get away, he would beat me."

"You couldn't use your fancy powers?"

"It's not like that," she said. "My power is time."

"What you mean?"

She stepped forward again. Eli didn't move.

"I'm the reason you kept seeing us over and over. I wanted you to see us. I kept going back in time. It's a time bend."

"Bullshit." Eli had yet to lower the gun. He took an examination of her face. Soft features, mostly in the center, making it seem rounder, childlike. Maybe that was the ruse. Innocence. That was the trap.

"Prove it—" Eli realized the gun had taken to trembling as if the metal was repelled by his skin. It rattled gently, hummed even. He was terrified. He grasped the gun with two hands and held tight.

"But you saw us! Over and over." The woman's voice pleaded but her eyes, those large round eyes, were dead.

"Ma'am, I just shot a man on account of you bein' roughed up, you're gon' need to give me a bit of a break here."

"You shot him because you were scared."

"No shit. I would've had a better shot had you not—"

"Let's see."

Black.

The driver bounded out of the car, baseball bat in full swing, rolling it in his hands.

The woman screamed and ran to the back of the toll shelter. "Please stop! Help! Help! Oh God!"

Eli was mystified. Back where it all went wrong. His mind connected and sparked into play.

"I'll shoot you!" Eli staggered back to his feet.

"I'd rather have *you* kill me, at least you won't tear me apart."

The driver continued to swing. Eli kicked at his chest and slipped.

"You just made the biggest mistake, buddy. Now she's going to kill all of us!"

The woman stood inside the shelter, just behind Eli. "He's lying!"

Eli was startled. "I said stay around the back!"

The woman ran to the back of the shelter and hid behind a small desk. The driver took a swing at Eli's ribs and connected. Eli tried to point his gun at the driver. Again, the driver kicked it out of his hand. Eli was face down, again.

I didn't get it right.

The ticker in his brain was still rattling. The driver kicked Eli in the face and entered the shelter through the plastic vertical blinds, stepping over his body.

"Come here, you little bitch. You can't hide from me. You wanna kill me? Come on!"

The woman emerged from behind the small desk in the middle of the tiny room. Once more.

"You don't know what you're doing. I won't harm you."

"You won't harm me? I just saw you destroy three people! And for what?"

Eli stood behind the driver and fired, killing him. It felt different —dutiful this time. But he'd made the same mistakes. He slipped. He got distracted.

No scream. This time, the woman didn't scream.

"Holy shit." Eli finally lowered the gun and looked at her skeptically.

"You still kicked him," the woman said.

"What?" The ticker in his brain finally slowing to a stop.

"If you hadn't kicked him, you could've shot him sooner."

"I didn't want to shoot him." Eli rubbed the back of his wet neck. He stared at the man, now haloed in crimson like a panic button. The woman stepped forward.

"Your face." She reached out to touch but recoiled.

"What about my face?" Eli slumped down in the office chair stationed in front of the small tv on the desk and wiped at the dried blood on his lips. The woman cautiously stepped closer, her eye on the gun still planted firmly in Eli's hand.

"You're not bleeding anymore," she said.

"Oh yeah." Eli crumpled upon himself even further. "About that."

The woman leaned on the desk. Eli clicked the safety back on and slipped it into his pocket. He planted both hands on the table. The woman exhaled slowly at the sight of the disappearing gun. Earnest. Bare. He might as well have raised his hands. The jig was up.

"You too?" she asked.

"Yes ma'am. I s'pose so."

"Always?" She tickled the desk nervously with her fingers.

"Ever since I was a little boy. I was a fast healer, broke over a dozen bones, healed that night."

"How wonderful for you." She glanced quickly at his holster.

"Only wonderful when nobody knew about it. My mama wasn't one for wall flowerin' and she liked the neighbors chattin' about her. She used to hold little shows where she'd give me a papercut, and everyone would watch it heal."

"I'm so sorry." Her eyes fixated on his holster. His eyes somewhere far away, reaching light years beyond the tiny desk. Beyond the television, beyond Kelly LeBrock.

"It's nothing."

"Does anyone know?" The woman's expression softened, her features with added years now, more angular, less cherubic than before and steadily, the lines in her forehead surfaced.

"No. Would you like some help, ma'am?"

"Orsha."

"Sorry?"

"My name is Orsha."

"Would you like some help, Orsha?"

"With?"

Eli stood from the desk with stamina mustered from some depth. Orsha's hands instinctively went up. He took a deep inhale, running his hands over her from a distance of a few inches. Deft precision, his fingers plucking the air. Her cuts closed quickly, like a peeping neighbor who'd been spotted. Bruises fading into pink skin, blood pulling itself back into the body, heading back to circulate once more. Eli stumbled, almost falling over the desk.

"I'm sorry! I haven't done that in years."

"It's fine. Thank you." Orsha stood in wonder, flexing her hands and arms, feeling her face.

"Where did he find you?" Eli glanced back over to the driver, who lay wide-eyed.

Orsha stepped forward, past Eli and towards the driver.

"I'd gone for a run and was headed home from the park when a car almost hit me as I was crossing the road. I stopped it. With my bare hands. A dead stop at forty miles an hour. Everyone inside the car bounced forward, hard. The man busted through the windshield, the woman shot sideways into the doorframe head first, the child"—she inhaled sharply—"the child, out the back. I saw him in his car watching me with terror. He followed me into my garage and knocked me out. Woke up in the back of his car."

"He was gonna sell you? To who?"

"I don't know. That's what he said on the phone to someone. Highest bid, he'll be there in a few hours. Guess they'll be waiting."

"Or come lookin.' Did you always have it? The car stop thing?"

Eli traced her silhouette with his eyes. Her body had become rounder, tighter, smoother in places he didn't notice before. He stopped himself and sheepishly looked down.

"I guess. Found out the first time I didn't want to come inside to play. Didn't realize that when I stopped it, no one else could play either. As I got older, I learned to just rewind." She walked closer to the driver, leaned down.

"Doesn't that make it harder, ma'am, eh, Orsha? To keep playing it?"

"I'm not really good at goodbyes so, yes I guess it does in the grand scheme of things." She stood and turned to Eli, a slight smile finding her lips. "They told us, your—our kind—that we were America's first line of defense. They revered us."

Eli saluted.

Orsha stifled a giggle and turned her gaze to the floor. "Until Article 1892."

"Fuck that thing. Strip our rights? Can't get decent jobs, outcast? All because of some idiot prejudice." Eli threw up his hands.

Orsha gestured around the room. "On today of all days. Huh, America's big night."

"It's Independence Day, not night."

"You don't know?" Orsha moved closer to Eli. "The Fourth of July. The Inhuman Purge. It's been online for weeks. Highest bidder, highest catch, highest death toll."

Eli slumped back down in the office chair. "Christ. I don't keep up with those things." He pointed to the stack of late eighties films on the desk. Orsha sighed and looked back at the driver.

"What're we going to do about him?"

"I don't rightly know."

"Thank you for saving me." Orsha reached out her hand for a shake. Eli didn't grasp it.

"I saved myself too, let's not forget that. But you're welcome." He reluctantly grasped her fingers, a shake like a limp fish.

"May I?" Orsha stood closer.

"May you what?" Eli stepped back on one of his heels.

Orsha reached out to hug him. He slowly brought her in. A fly in the room buzzed loudly around them.

Eli caught sight of it as it hung in time, suspended, the buzz low and droning. He clasped his hand around her waist as she hung on to him, on his neck, tighter than she needed to, eyes closed.

Click.

A shot rang out. The woman dropped and the fly began to circle again. Eli sat back down in his office chair and started to clean the gun meticulously. He placed two more bullets in the chamber, wiped it down with a handkerchief and placed it back under the duct tape, behind the stack of videos. He took a quick assessment of the scene. The driver, the woman, and the fly still circling. He reached for his walkie-talkie. "Cresthill, do you copy, please?" Static. Finally, a voice scattered in from the other end.

"Copy Fly on the Wall, we hear you."

"Yes, evening boys, I've got myself a Code 6. Two dead, one inhuman."

"Dead inhuman?" The voice poised in interest.

"Yessir, unfortunately it struggled, and I mortally wounded it." Eli looked at Orsha. She was face up, features softer once again. The cherub and the driver. Like Mercutio and Tybalt, lying on the streets of Verona, with a mere fly between them.

"Good work, Fly on the Wall. We admire your bravery. We'll arrive soon for our collection. Thank you for keeping these filthy vermin off our streets."

"To America." Eli saluted to no one.

"To America!" A crackle on the other end. A dead signal hissed in Eli's ear. Pushing aside the deteriorating DVD cases, he took another look at the two passengers. He placed the walkie talkie in his pocket and lay down on his desk and began to cry.

Wiping his face with his hands and pushing them onto the thighs of his pants, he pushed play on *Weird Science* again.

The sky was turning into a Sedona landscape. Blues, pink and subtle oranges filled the horizon. Peace. Birds made their way in Vshapes along the last hints of the Cheshire cat grin of a moon still hanging in the air. A low rumble took Eli's attention away from the serene setting. Thrust back into the dust, blood, and bronze of the night before.

Three black SUVs were lined up at the checkpoint. Men in Hazmat suits placed the woman in the white body bag with a plastic window. They placed her in a metal tube encased in the back of one of the SUVs. The driver was placed in a black body bag and put in a canister. He was placed in another SUV. A man in a black suit handed Eli a considerable sum of money in a manila envelope. Eli thumbed the bills and closed the envelope, nodding.

Two Hazmat men cleaned the shelter and outside spotless. Eli stood, contrite, out of the way. The men raked over the tracks of the Mustang as all the vehicles rolled back out of the exit. The Mustang was secured to the tow hitch on the last SUV. Eli straightened the place, turned the security camera off the loop, emptied the change except for one vehicle's worth and swept. An hour later, relief, at last.

A tall thin man with a big smile and orange vest. Pat Collins. He waved happily at Eli.

"How'd it go, out here in the boonies? It'd give me the creeps."

Eli pulled a shy grin out of nowhere. "Uneventful as always. Easy money."

"You got that right!" Pat playfully slapped Eli on the back.

Eli entered his worn-out 2004 Honda Civic and took the walkie talkie out of his pocket, placing it on the passenger seat. He ran his thumb over it for a few strokes then turned his attention to the glove compartment. He tossed the thick manila envelope in, and it scattered amongst the others. He pulled on his sunglasses.

With a good night's work done, Eli drove down the interstate.

Pat stood in the checkpoint shelter, mesmerized. With a crooked smile, he watched the statuesque woman in bikini underwear walk-dance on the TV screen. He mimicked the lines verbatim in tandem with the panty-clad woman.

"So, what would you little maniacs like to do first?"

Pride

If you could stand inside my head for two minutes, you'd feel like a heathen bothering me for anything. It always comes crashing down, just like I said it would, stinking and sordid. On me! Always, just on me. "It is what it is," they say. "It doesn't 'serve' you," they say. I say sod it and keep your damned new age fuckery.

—Lucas Duncan (Brain Book, 2017)

Eager

Memo 1

Let's call this one *The Jelly Dance*.

"You can't be fucking serious."

That's been my motto for the last six undignified years. My name is Lucas Duncan, and my life is falling apart. I'd had fancy training, early days treading the board, writing award-winning films and television.

Dust. Dust in the palm of my fucking hand. I suppose it's best to take you back to the beginning. Not six years, mind you. Just to where the bottom began to drop out completely. Before I forget everything, before I couldn't function, and as they say: stick with me, my story gets better.

In the spring of 2017, I had taken to scribbling all my impure, rude, and less qualified thoughts into a Moleskine notebook no bigger than an index card. I figured that way, I could keep composure when all I really wanted to do was kick someone's face in. Well, not everyone, but most of the producers, showrunners, directors, agents, and any other bureaucratic blowhard who told me, "It just isn't the right time for this piece," or "I think we'll unfortunately pass." Did I mention I'd gone through nineteen of these notebooks in the last six months? I'm wearing thin here, crazier than a shithouse rat. Death is inevitable, or is it enviable? I can't break apart the two at this point.

It wasn't always this way. I'm really even-keeled, actually. In the right situations with the right people, I'm a downright joy. The thing is, I couldn't even get in front of people these days. Friendships were running out of gas, and relationships? Christ, relationships. Offers had dried up, new and "Up and Coming" infants took my place on rosters, stages, writers' rooms. Some of those newbies I'd brought into the business.

My father would call that "A fine how do you do." I call it biting the hand that feeds you. It happened more and more, hence the upswing in notebook purchases. It became more of a diary of sorts, I guess. I've taken to dating it, trying to find some sort of sign where it all went wrong. A collection of ideas, to-dos, colorful language, and the odd old-timey adage thrown in.

Let's see, May 10th:

Honestly, you ruddy faced asshole—

Milk, special expensive chicken and rice mixture for ungrateful dog

Spendthrift is a good word

It was if the magic had stirred something angelic about her, some glimpse of youthful naivete between the cracks of…

If this leaky bag so much as touches me, I swear to God.

Utter madness.

May 11th. I was clearly feeling overly anxious.

GET YOUR FUCKING PURSE OUT THE GOD DAMN DOOR SO IT WILL CLOSE!

Just one Cornetto, give it to me, delicious ice cream, from Italy.

Waldorf Salad looks like the dog got into the garbage.

This better not be another meeting that could have just been a rejection call.

Find those chocolate melting cakes, carrots. For balance.

Your friend isn't listening anymore, woman, can it.

I've only put deodorant under one arm. And now it's noticeable.

The anxiety grasped me that fine day in May, a day that will live in indignity, as I was on my way to meet with Jimmi. With an 'i' on the end, can you imagine? Like a twelve-year-old girl. He was new to my agency's office as an actor's rep, and I'd been mostly needing that since the writing gigs took a turn for the dearth back in '15. He'd taken over for Carol, the big boss's assistant, when she got a divorce and it got messy. Carol moved to the country. Nerves, they said.

Anyway, Jimmi was the one I was counting on, as Nancy—my current agent—was busy with her new up-and-comers. We'd been together for fifteen years and after a while I much appreciated the minimal-maintenance relationship. But like I said, Jimmi.

Jimmi was trying to help me, well—how do I paraphrase this to where I don't get pissed off? He was helping to scrape the twenty-year-old mold off my "flaccid" career. *Flaccid*, he said. But like an idiot, I was looking for any injection of life. Anything at all.

So, I sat on the train and scribbled nonsense for thirty-five minutes. Yes. All that gibberish on the page in just thirty-five minutes. I've spared you my tirade of the endless shopping bags and baguettes in my face as I tried to make it past a party of tourists, the shit I stepped in rounding the corner—I still cannot decipher which species it was from—and the poorly-made concoction of my simple request of a Vodka tonic.

Thirty-five minutes laid between me and a silver lining. But though I had hoped for a shift out of mundane aging writer/actor-ville, I got nothing but bungle.

"Scotch? Seventeen years old." Jimmi asked. In his pinstripe suit, bullshit grin, and clean-shaven over-sized head, he looked like Bond villain cosplay.

"No. No thank you." I waved it away. My stomach was in knots already that morning, and I hadn't eaten. Incidentally, I was planning to get drunk anyway after that meeting, no matter which way it went.

"I want you to picture a place where you risk it all." Jimmi took off his suit jacket, then pointed at me. I was used to this, the first indication of the fact you're about to swim in bullshit.

"Risk it all? Jimmi, I'm not sure I could even liquidize the 'all' that I don't have. Get to the point."

"Fine, I'll skip the seduction," he said. "How do you feel— about a national television spot?"

"Fucking hell, wow! Oh wait, it's not the God-awful cruise line ones where Chev Sanders does the conga line, is it?"

I bloody hated Chev Sanders. His teeth had been capped to the size of mini marshmallows.

Jimmi went on with the seduction he'd promised to skip.

"Better! Think of something for everyone. Think juicy. Think after a grueling day wouldn't you want a—"

"Pint! I'm the new 'most interesting man in the world,' aren't I?" I was honestly almost on my feet, but Nancy had told me that agents secretly hate it when you're excited about everything. It makes you *and* them seem like anyone could coax you in any direction with a porkchop.

"Uh no. Frandelheins wants you to be their new spokesperson."

"Frandelheins?"

"Yes."

Fucking jellybeans. Fucking overly processed, floss-baiting, fake fruit like nothing on the planet jellybeans. I didn't know whether to scream, cry, sit back in my chair, or flip his desk. On account of an actor charging into the office once with a toy gun after he was unceremoniously cut from a role in *A Thousand Summers*, a low budget daytime soap, my only coping mechanism was stuffed in the side pocket of my bag, held hostage at the reception desk upfront.

"Why?" I was baffled.

"Because they wanna make jellybeans more sophisticated again."

He said "again" like jellybeans were ever the damn Cary Grant of the candy world. I let him continue, mostly because my mouth was as dry as a sarcophagus.

"You know how Jelly Belly went on with all of those exciting flavors? Well, Frandelheins wants to take it one step further, but for adults. Flavors like Champagne, Beef Bourguignon, Crème Caramel, Pâté."

"Jimmi, no one, like, *no one* wants to dig through a bag of jellybeans for the pâté ones when they can just go and buy a fuck off tub of pâté!"

I felt hot and I didn't realize not only the bellow, but the octave of my voice rose. Now I'd done it. Jimmi raised an eyebrow and leaned his head back. He observed the ceiling for what felt like decades and then spun on his heels and turned his back to me, dramatically straightening pictures and accolades along his walls.

"Lucas, you're a smart man. No slouch in talent, looks—well, a little nip here, a little follicle graft in the back."

I beg your pardon, you tube of Vaseline squeezed into an Italian suit. My God! My Moleskine. I was almost salivating waiting to touch it.

"Does this anti-flattery have a point?" I wasn't going to go down without a dash of vinegar.

"Frandelheins thinks you're a sophisticated man of a certain age."

"I'm forty-seven."

"Precisely. They want debonair, charm, talent. All those things you can't get with a twenty-five-year-old *Big Brother* cast-off with six-pack abs. You're fit enough for what they want you to do."

I literally couldn't move. I couldn't tell if I'd just been flirted with or insulted. The lines were so blurred, I couldn't keep track.

"Thank you? And precisely what is it they'd like me to do? Sit at a desk in a tuxedo drinking Chandon? Slowly savoring a pâté jellybean in quiet ecstasy?"

"No. They'd like you to be one."

Fuck.

"I'm sorry?"

You can't be fucking serious.

"They'd like you to dress up as the Champagne jellybean."

"Enough!! You lure me in here with the promise of dusting off my career and you try to feed me Humphrey Bogart in a goddamned jelly suit?"

I had no idea how long I'd been standing, and I was startled to find I'd smashed something. I was also holding the scotch. My hand throbbed to fling it across the room, as if I hadn't been dramatic already. But my brain had a target for Jimmi, and it flew, hitting Jimmi square in the nose.

There was a loud scream, almost guttural. Sending—Sophie, Sophia, or Sandra, I couldn't remember—flying in. I was panting and standing over Jimmi like some bird of prey. I remembered the notebook and dashed into reception to retrieve it before Jimmi lunged to his feet.

"You'll never work in this town again, you prick! I'm suing the hell out of you! I'll take everything!"

The joke's on Jimmi: my ex-wife Diana took "everything" years ago. But he wasn't lying. I most likely would never work in this town again, not if anyone in this industry saw to it.

It was a sheer downpour as I headed out of the office. From across the street, I saw a vision that made my heart ache, and my joints lock up. Maria. Busily typing away in La James coffeehouse. Maria was a marvelous misstep I'd taken at the wrong time. I wasn't ready for anything serious, and I'd forgotten to mention that. I squinted and relaxed when I saw what I needed, her left ring finger was free of any jewelry. I trembled as the cold and wet started to sting and got out of there quickly as she raised her head. I grabbed my bag tight to my chest, and I realized I'd torn a strap jerking it out from under what's-her-faces' chair. And then it hit me: I'd have to do what I've never done. Beg for an honest-to-God, real fucking job.

Memo 2

Let's call this one *The Man from New York*.

My mate Dennis had it made. Eclectic pub owner, side gig playing drummer in a house band in an amazing jazz club across town, and a sweet, no-frills lady. He was also a giant, a family trait. We'd been the same height all through junior school until one summer he shot up a third of a meter leaving me in the dust. In old pictures I looked like a footstool to the rest of Den's family— skyscrapers, every single one.

I'd stopped for a chat that day and well, as I said, I was planning to get drunk anyway. As I stepped into Tinker's, a thought rushed into me like a bitter wind. I honestly could not remember the last time my life was that easy or happy. I'd settle for remotely pleasurable.

Now, I'm not saying things were easy for Den per se, but I do suppose I was a bit jealous that things for him always seemed remotely pleasurable. So why did I put myself through the torture of the mental compare-and-contrast? Main reason, he was a top-notch person, second, he was the only one who answered the phone those days.

"You look like a soggy sandwich!" Dennis was not only a redwood of a man but had a booming voice to match. And with that, most of the patrons turned in the direction of the soggy sandwich.

I took off my jacket and shook it out by the door and proceeded to hang it on the furthest hanger away from the rest. You know, courtesy.

"You're a sonofabitch. How's the day?" I sidled onto a stool and skidded a bit, remembering that my backside was completely wet. I went with it as I was in no mood to budge further.

"Eh, it's alright. Bit busier with the rain now. Why didn't you take the train, Lucas? You look a mess."

"Thank you. And I couldn't bring myself to get onto another train today, honestly, people this week. My skin is crawling." It had been on pins and needles for at least a month, the doctor said it was nerves. Nerves I knew I had, and I could have paid myself 175 quid to figure that out.

"Well, I'm glad you got to take the martyr's walk in the rain to wash the stench of the common people off ya. Hell, don't you ever get tired of being tired?"

Den always meant well but he could be a real cunt sometimes. I'm sorry. I shouldn't have said that. He crossed his arms and leaned into me. Partially annoyed, partially concerned. He got my goat most of the time. But I trusted him. I digress.

I'd propped my bag between my feet on the "ladies' ledge," as Den's wife called it. So ladies' feet don't dangle at the height of the stools. It's ruined. Fancy rucksack style, oiled leather, now a soggy pile.

"No, I don't, Den, and I'll tell you why. Do you realize that it has been five years since I have had anything catch, Den? Five whole years. I head to most meetings with the verve I'd head into a dentist with."

"Well maybe that's why, you're too smug from the start."

"I wish. Most times it's a notes meeting, just to tell me how much they'd change *if* they were going to push it, then by the end of the meeting it's a full pass. Like, what the hell, you couldn't tell me that over the phone? And furthermore, at least two of these gatekeeping snakes were understudies in *Charlotte and the Great Dance.* Can you imagine? I broke records with that play! And now these nauseously unqualified brats are telling *me* that it's a full pass."

"Things change Lucas, obviously they're not taking your road anymore and found something that they feel they can thrive in. After all, you said they're young. Who wants to be an understudy for twenty years?"

"You're not taking their side!"

"I'm not taking anyone's side. And I've been around, Lucas, I know how long it's been, and Diana sure didn't help."

I shuddered and my mind drifted. No, Diana didn't help. It should have been a cut and dry divorce, fifteen years, no kids. No real mutual financial hang-ups. But it got slanderous and petty— fast. The person you've shared a good deal of your formative life getting to know, loving, sharing a house with, looks at you one day and says, "Meh, it was alright."

I'd married Diana after a run we both starred in. The wise older woman with legs up to her neck. And me, the peevish man-boy who saw nothing but stars and all-night romps when I looked at her, and she obliged enthusiastically on the latter account. And after the years, the honeymoon stage wore off and I was no longer young but all the more man-boy, it disintegrated. Our life of exotic vacations and hideous world collectibles were the envy of our friend circle. So, I suppose for window dressing only, we hung on for another fifteen years.

She was unmoved, didn't care if I was there or a million miles away. I had become part of the furniture. But when I decided to leave, tail firmly between legs, she took me to the cleaners. And all of those "no real mutual financial hang-ups" came pouring out of the woodwork. I pulled my Moleskine out of my side pocket with fear and gritted teeth. It was dry, thank God. I shoved it in my inside jacket pocket.

At that moment, Den turned to leave me, and just like that, my mini counselling session was over. I moved on to the liquid psychiatrist: whiskey. Den's wife Rebecca lets me drink for free.

I racked my brain trying to get back to where it all started to relax a bit. That place where I heard my first few noes in a row. I took them in stride. "You can't shine all the time," I used to say. And I was still busy then. But now I was being bled dry— personally and professionally. So, I've just been this husk waiting for someone to see me alive and kicking. But not as a goddamned jelly.

Rebecca came through to fill my glass for the second time, a tall pour, reaching the rim. Atta girl. I winked. She rolled her eyes. I swallowed this last one hard and it burned in just the right spot. One more and I could go home, eat my weight in Walker's, feed the dog, and go to bed. And I should've just left then.

As I set down my glass, I noticed a man in my peripheral vision, seated on the next stool. Was I already drunk? How long had he been there? Poor sod. He had the same look I did. He caught me staring, and like an idiot I didn't turn away. I just looked like a child who'd gotten caught stealing something. My eyes widened.

"You get caught in the rain too?" he asked. Middle-aged man, olive skin, deep lines, and a mammoth head of hair.

Follicle graft. Jimmi, you pissant.

"Yes, train was full, so I said screw it, it's only seven blocks. And then the skies opened up."

He sipped his drink and chuckled. "Mother Nature, you never know what she's up to. My mother was like that, turn on my father in a second. Lovey-dovey to putting glass in your salad like that." He snapped his fingers in my face, startling me. My wet ass squeaked in my chair, and he laughed loudly.

"McNicky." He was American, amazingly jovial and for some odd reason I wasn't recoiling. Oh, it's not the American thing, it's the people thing. I haven't been able to stand them recently. But this fella seemed alright.

"I'm sorry?"

"Mike McNicky, from Queens."

"Lucas Duncan, the gutter."

"Shit, this isn't gonna be a down on your luck story, is it?" He rolled his eyes.

Well. Misjudged that one.

"Well, not necessarily but—" He slapped me hard with the back of his hand on my shoulder.

"Well good, cause I was gonna tell one." His boisterous laugh was oddly endearing. I laughed too, genuinely giggled, unforced for the first time in about a year.

"Well then," I said. "Please do go on."

He waved his hand then pointed at me in gun mime. "Nah, looks like you need all the help you can get, and I see you're a few glasses into your therapy session, so get it out before you topple over."

He was right, that second one went down so well. I had noticed the room jiggled a bit. I flagged Rebecca for a water. She gave me the finger.

"Well, to be quite honest, Mike—"

He raised his hand. "McNicky, please. On account of I'm a junior and my father is a sneaky sonofabitch. Continue. My apologies."

I stuttered, collecting my thoughts. Goddamn it, he was fabulous. Out of some mid-70s gangster tale.

"I—I was saying that today, I may have just ruined my already shit-stained career. I threw a decanter of scotch at my agent's assistant."

"Fuck, man! Didn't get the assailant vibe from you. More Hemingway but wetter. Over what?"

"I'm sorry?"

"Why'd you throw the scotch?"

"Hmm." The world turned for a moment and I supposed there were a million reasons why. But my dearest Mr. McNicky, you could not understand.

In the last few years, I'd left my wife, who'd drained me dry emotionally, mentally, and financially. Which begged to state, had also destroyed me physically. I took a shine to a lovely young lady so out of my league and completely undeserving of my malaise and self-deprecating vitriol that I had to throw the whole relationship in the bin. I had to downgrade my apartment—twice. Which was fine, but the dog couldn't do a once-around without knocking into the four corners of the house. The fear and anxiety had taken such hold that it was a toss-up if I'd wake up screaming or I'd be unable to sleep because I was quite sure I was having a heart attack. I'd started having debilitating panic attacks that reduced me to uncontrollable tears—blubbering tears. Thank God I lived alone. But I kept it simple for him.

"Where do I even begin? Divorce, dead writing and acting career, one silver lining."

"Silver linings are good, but make sure it ain't just tin foil." His boisterous laugh struck again.

I looked around and no one noticed this time, which was good because I was enjoying our little one on one. I spun to realize Rebecca had left me ice water. That gem of a woman.

"True, very true." The first sip was magic, I also began to realize how sober I wasn't. I continued.

"The silver lining is there is a shithole play that was given to me by a friend that I'd revised to a real juicer of a role. I'm happy to try the stage again, anything to keep my career out of the toilet. I'm happy to circle the bowl for a while. Even if it's in a tiny play in a tiny playhouse. Hopefully, it'll catch."

"Wow, artistic, are we? Sounds like things could look up. What makes you happier? Writing or acting?"

I leaned my head back to think, and the intoxicated equilibrium shift made me drift off in thought.

Fuck. I don't know, McNicky. Both are equally satisfying. Acting was my first love. My formative life was less than easy. My father was a bit of a functioning alcoholic, my mother was less than sensitive to any kind of emotional outburst. So, it was so exciting and refreshing to get to be someone or something else. I dove into it. I couldn't wait to be someone else. Writing, I guess, was the same way? I suppose. I could create anything and get these borderline-psychotic thoughts out of my head and down on the page. Build a world which I could thrive in, be anything in. In constant identity crisis. Damn.

I was back with him, and it was clear I'd begun to slur. "Both, I suppose. They both give me an outlet to do exactly what I want. I enjoy creating. But really what gets me, and it didn't mean much until about a decade ago, is the accolades. The prestige. The fact that I meant something to someone. I was being sought after. Wanted."

"Ah yes. The fame, the praise. It'll do it for you. So, what happened to where the gutter is now your home?"

He'd leaned back a bit. Arms crossed behind his head with fingers latched. In front of him were four empty glasses. I didn't recall him ordering or even coming in. Maybe he snuck in while I was regaling Den. Something was a bit off and I felt antsy. I touched my chest, feeling for the weight of my notebook. Thank God, it was still there. I realized I was spilling at him here. Easily. And I couldn't tell you why. So I changed the subject. "You hadn't said what brought you to London."

"True. Work, unfortunately."

"Ah, you'd be better to not scoff at work around here these days. Its feast or famine for most vocations here."

"Oh, I'm sure. My boss, you see, told me I need to broaden my horizons. I'm a workaholic. He said a little rest might help me. But I gotta tell you, you can't take the worker bee too far from the hive."

"A little R&R so you can hit the ground running back home?"

"A bit like that."

Finally. A nugget. I was still not sure what it was about him, with which I was being incredibly patient. Almost hanging on his every word. As if some drop of wisdom was going to change my life.

"What's your line of work?" I clung tightly to the bar, my head was buzzing.

"You could say I'm a life coach."

"I could say?"

He stifled a laugh and unlatched his hands to sit forward. He leaned into me, looked me square in the eye, and sighed. "I am more than a life coach. I help people achieve their every desire."

Now I'd seen it. That Tony Robbins bullshit aura. Lured me in with the "tell me your troubles" line. "Ah, well, McNicky, I hope you help a few lost souls before you shuffle back to Queens."

"Dah! Everybody does that."

"Does what?"

"Gives me the bum's rush when I say that."

Well shit. I was in no mood to be someone's "aw there, there." I had more issues than—oh what the hell. "I'm sorry, but it seemed a bit of a swindle and I felt like a mark."

"Nah, nothing like that. But you do look like a sad sack."

Nice zinger, McNicky. "My every desire? Eh?"

"Not without hard work and following the process."

"Seven easy installments of £399?"

He bellowed again, the loudest so far. But this time, everyone was silent. I couldn't bear to look. I didn't dare lift my head. Den was going to kill me for this.

Memo 3

Let's call this one, *Outline. Engage. Embody.*

I chanced it. I turned to say a quick "Sorry, folks." But the words didn't come. They could not even be formed. I stood slowly, realizing how completely knackered I was. McNicky stood close behind me. He placed a hand on my shoulder, and I shuddered and backed away, knocking over a stool loudly.

The people. All the bustling, drinking, snogging, and talking people … were gone. Not a soul. No noise. No music. Just quiet. Eerie quiet, like the vacuum of air that greets you when you're trying to listen for the noise of someone possibly breaking into your home. McNicky broke the silence like a whipcrack.

"It's about time. What's a fella got to do to get everyone to shut up?"

This time he wheezed in laughter instead. He bent at the waist in hysterics. I was sick. Truly nauseous, and I lost it. All of it. Well, I'd mostly had a liquid diet that day. I checked my clothing for splatter and wiped my mouth. I stumbled to the bar for the water Rebecca had left. Still there. Cool and forgiving. Part of me was astonished, part of me was terrified, and the other part hoped he killed me.

"Lucas, I'm sorry, but we had to be alone."

"What have you done?"

"What have I done?" He was offended. He stuffed both hands in his pockets and inspected the ceiling. "I'm about to change your life, give you everything you desire, but I'm the bad guy? Me?"

I'd gone off the deep end. Finally cracked this time. Den had said, the week before this, that I looked haggard. Anguished. Rebecca had lovingly chimed in that she was wondering how I wasn't dead already.

Shit. I'm dead. I'm fucking dead. "Am I dead?" *Fuck, please don't let me be dead*, I prayed. Off my shit in my mate's pub, on the floor. A wonderful send off.

"Is that your greatest desire?"

"Fuck no!"

"Ha! Well okay then. Nothing to worry about there. Now I believe we can talk openly about what's really troubling you."

"What's there to know? I said all I've needed to. Now, please, Mr. McNicky, I'm not well and I'd really like to be home to my daft dog."

"What's your hurry? I'm not gonna kill ya, Luke."

"Lucas. On account of that's my fucking name."

McNicky sized me up. *Shit, I'm dead. I'm so dead.* I thought. And I realized if that was the true nature to my end, why I gave so much of a fuck about it. I'd always thought old age would get me. A long debilitating whatsit after I'd written my last great miniseries. I supposed it was just as well. What was funny was, with all the bitching and what not, I never thought I'd be given the option. I thought I'd live out the rest of my days until I drank myself to death like my old man.

I stumbled. Haphazardly, I moved throughout the bar like some injured animal. I fell hard over something. A sweater. No doubt in someone's hand and fallen to the floor as they vanished. I yanked it from around my ankle and tossed it wildly, as if it were alive.

"Lucas, I'm going to need you to sit."

"Why?" I was crawling now. A metallic taste took over my tongue. There was blood in my mouth from the fall. I felt around for all my teeth. Winner, winner. Fantastic. I heard McNicky behind me.

"Lucas get up, you're embarrassing yourself."

"In front of whom? You've already killed everyone!"

"I've killed no one. They're all still here."

"Why me?"

"Why not you, Lucas?"

I'd already given up. Instinctively, I gave McNicky my hand. He helped me to my feet. Jesus, I was drunk. Rebecca pours six ounces instead of two, and neat at that. Sometimes I love her. That night, I could've strangled her.

"McNicky, tell me, honestly. What the hell is going on here? I'm hoping you're a figment or a hallucination. Oh God, you're a hallucination, aren't you? A little absinthe, eh, Rebecca?" I was shouting. That was four times now, that day alone, that I didn't realize I was shouting. Nerves.

"Lucas, sit, please."

I found the nearest stool, sat, and squeaked, and wondered how my ass was still wet. McNicky approached me slowly.

"Lucas, I want to tell you a little bit about my vocation." He darted around, startled by the ice shifting in a glass. "I've been around for an awfully long time; this game of Life is not new to me. And I've had my share of disappointments and mistakes. But I was given this little vacation to … how do you say, take the edge off. Now, that being said, my job is helping people achieve anything they want by simply wishing it so. No deviation, just headlong into the fucker, you understand?"

I wiped my soggy nose. "No."

"Fine, you will. Lucas, there's always a recurring string of actions in people's lives that make them who they are. Heartache. Death. Wounded pride, et cetera."

He paced. What was odd, outside of the fact that I was certain I was in clear and present danger of being expired, is that his vernacular kept changing. Soft-spoken one moment, Old Quincy from Queens the next. I was being put on. But by whom, and by what exactly I couldn't confirm. I was incapable of movement or sound, so he continued, unchallenged.

"This string follows them around like a leash. And every now and again, someone steps on that leash and jerks you back. Now, you either defend yourself or keep it moving. Most people defend themselves, and that is what they carry for life. The cycle of self-preservation. That sweet bubble that no one gets in, and you never get out of. And that is what keeps people from achieving everything they desire. Can people free themselves from this bubble? Of course. 99.9 percent of people do not want to do that."

"Maybe you just couldn't care less about what people think anymore."

"Oh Lucas, you and I both know that doesn't describe you, my friend."

I was either dead drunk or hallucinating, but halos of bodies twinkled in and out, like the sunspots on your eyes as you make your way back inside from a day with no shade. "You were saying?"

"Age nine, the sea, the tide came in hard and swift that day. Your brother got a mouthful of sand going ass over tea kettle in it and choked."

I was closer to McNicky now. Walked, I supposed, or was carried by the terror of that horrible afternoon. "Yes, he got swept out a-ways. I was running, trying to grab him. I'd caught him by the leg but lost my grip. A man in the water grabbed him and brought him out."

"They revived him, yeah? He was alright?"

"Yeah, he took a big gulp of water and the sand got in, we took him to the hospital."

"Your parents must have been very proud of your bravery that day."

They hadn't. My father said nothing all the way to the hospital. Just gave me side glances of disappointment. My mother had ridden with Charles in the ambulance.

"When I met my mother and Charles at the hospital, he was having a popsicle. Right as rain. My mother took me outside of the room. I'll never forget it. She knelt on one knee and placed her hands on my shoulders."

"What did she say?"

"She said, 'Lucas, do you know why we're here?' I said, 'Yes, because Charles fell in the water.' She said, 'No, we're here because little fat boys aren't fast enough to save their brothers from drowning.' Then she stood, as stiff as she knelt, and walked back into Charles' room."

Outside of old pictures with me jockeying on her lap at two years old, and the neighborly church greeting of peace mid-sermon, I couldn't quite recall my mother laying comforting hands on me again after that.

I supposed I'd drifted again. McNicky clapped his hands together. "Age twenty-five, packed house. Common's Theatre. *Lifeline*. Seventh night. The line was?" McNicky said.

Fucks sake. Not this. Why was he doing this? Ghost of Christmas ruddy Past with this one. That night at Common's was the driest night of my life. I'd worked so hard to be off book even before the audition and I'd done it. Much to the chagrin of Felix, the fuck-sucking goofball that became my understudy.

"I'm a creature of habit, Florence. Would you think me a tiger in your bed? Or a butterfly flitting about your face?"

"Why couldn't you say it? Seems easy enough."

"Because I had dumped the girl who played Florence the day before."

"Lucas, you animal."

"It was revenge, really. I'd tried cutting her off once before, but we'd made a go of it again because she was pregnant. And all I could think of was, honestly, *not now*. I can't be a father, let alone a father with a woman who had not only drained my patience but drove most of my mates away. Turned out that it was a lie, so as soon as I found out, I cut it off for good. Of course she was upset, but she had made this move, this mime, where she cradled her belly like a mother, right before my line. So, I blanked and improvised the line, throwing off the next three cues and the entire first act. It was salvaged enough, but what a blemish. Felix played the next three nights, and of course got saddled with the glamour-boy status of saving the show. My flake was on industry night."

McNicky circled me. *Sure, open me up and then finish me off.* Diana was a master at that. Wearing me down with inane arguments and then, just as I was making sense of it all, she'd hit me with a curveball. Something quite cutting and angry. Then days upon days of stroppy attitude until I apologized. *I* fucking apologized for her getting angry with *me* for disproving her argument.

McNicky was right. I was a sad sack. I hoped he would kill me.

"When did it start feeling good, this praise? No offense, but you're bringing me down here."

"I suppose it was when I played Samuel in *All There Is*. Everything clicked. All of it. From being on book to closing night. And not that superficial, fake it 'til you make it bullshit. The real deal. I was fantastic."

"Well of course. Got the bug then?"

"Nah, I'd had it before. Everything felt like filler before then. Like timewasters."

"Ahh, the golden goose. The fucker that sent you sky-high."

"Yes, uh—" A vomitous burp erupted in my throat.

"Well then, what happened after that?"

"Everything. I got cast in ninety percent of what I read for, sometimes multiple stints of the same play in different countries. I started film work, TV. I'd been asked to write a few episodes for shows I adored. Everything came in an avalanche. I met Diana around then too."

"Then why can't you do it again? What's stopping you from having another fucker like that?"

"People stopped caring. My ideas for my own pieces were too contrived, too out there. There's always notes on 'how to improve.' Eventually the phone stopped ringing."

"All I hear is a bunch of 'aw shucks, doesn't it suck to be me.'"

Well shit, McNicky, at the moment, it does. He saw the pity in my face, and I was actually ashamed. I closed my eyes for a moment and took a gulp of air and there it was. The aroma of a Cuban cigar and hair pomade. He was in my face, like a cat trying to wake you by staring into your soul. "Get your ass up! This is fucking ridiculous. You mean to tell me people stopped liking you and you said OKAY?"

"They didn't like my work. My fucking day-to-day work, it's not like I can pick up some hours at the office like—"

"Oh, like some old working stiff, God forbid, poor fucking Lucas."

"I don't fucking need this. You're a stranger who's drugged me and dissected me and now I want—" Retch. The sick hung out in the back of my throat like a dry pill. I don't think I'd ever been so relieved about vomiting.

"You were saying, Lucas?"

I was over it. Half-moaning, I begged him to stop. "What do you want, McNicky?"

"I want you to want to be successful again."

"You fucking think *I* don't?"

"No, you wanna be a sad sack, because if you didn't have a moan or a self-deprecating joke, what would you do with your day? It's your fault you are where you are."

This sonofabitch was—right. I'd had an easy time traipsing out the "poor me" routine. It got sympathy, pats on the back, the occasional shag. Man alive, I'd been tagged. The mask had been harder to hold onto than a car on a hairpin turn.

"You mean to tell me you have zero, zero prospects at another golden goose?"

"Well, there's that play."

"The shithole play?"

Fuck he was good. "Yes. The shithole play."

"Well, you re-wrote the fucker, now get on your way and audition. This! This is destiny. This is the mutha. Why don't you want it bad enough?"

"Because it's a shithole."

"Was. Was a shithole but these hands, this talent …" He poked me hard in the chest and then grasped my wrists. Reminiscent of my mother making the pre-dinner wash check. "These hands have made so many dreams and fantasies and arguments and kisses and damages come to life. I bet they made that shithole sing. Eh?"

"Fine. Fine, yes, you're right. I cleaned it up, quite a bit."

"Outline. Engage. Embody. Repeat."

"I'm sorry?"

"Say it with me, Lucas."

"Outline. Engage. Embody. Repeat."

Over and over, our voices got louder. I was frenzied and alert. Ambitious and itchy. He grabbed my forearm, so it was parallel to his and pulled me toward him. Our eyes squared to each other, it was like an electric shock through me.

"Lucas, are you ready to claim your destiny?"

"I'm ready!"

"For what?"

Den looked at me mystified. I was off it. Knackered and wired at the same time. The bar was cleared out. Not a sign of McNicky or my retching. And the drunk was not only back, but in full force.

Apparently, the sauce had caught up, and I was forced to reconcile what it was I was actually doing on the planet anymore.

Sure, I'd thought about it, the great beyond. Knife to wrist even. Chicken-shitted out. I'd lost it now. I'd imagined a fully formed and functional human being, with a swagger and dialect I could've only hoped to create in my next spaghetti western. And as he came, a figment. And as he left, a puff of smoke.

Smoke. I rubbed my forehead with my sleeve. The faint whiff of a Cuban cigar. *Go to bed, mate. Enough poison for one night.* One night that showed me how far off the deep end I'd actually fallen. A voice came and a body followed. McNicky. My imagination was gold.

I'd Uber'ed home, apparently—said the bank alert on my phone that flashed angrily, along with the twenty-two text messages, fourteen missed calls from Nancy, and one from Hammonds and Creek Law Firm. I left Alim, the driver, five stars for not engaging with a man who'd seen a ghost. Or had I? I was so cold and clammy at that point, I was unsure if I was real. I wondered if I'd been slipped something, had turned away for a split second. I was at a loss.

Few things prepare the mind as it races through what could be a mental breakdown. Over the last twenty-four hours of May 11th, I had not been able to control the volume of my voice, I'd assaulted a man, and I'd seen what I can only believe was a figment so real, I distinctly remembered the smell of his breath: an odd mix of warm whiskey and the stale smear of a communion wafer. I took stock of everything, absolutely everything over the last few years. What had gone wrong, what had gone right—and I brushed that aside, because I could manage wrong. Right takes more concentration, more time. I never felt I had any. And maybe now I didn't.

Was I to believe that Mr. McNicky was some sort of post-modern Jacob Marley? Bah humbug to the smug sonofabitch. If anything, he'd got me thinking. What was I waiting for? I thrusted my laptop open to print the best rewrite of a shitstorm play this world has ever seen. But not just yet.

Updating.

You can't be fucking serious.

Memo 4

Let's call this *Songbird*.

I didn't use the Moleskine at all the next morning. Oddly, I felt quite light. *Outline. Embody. Engage.* Maybe it was McNicky's spirit driving me. Maybe I was just very attuned to the fact that I'd be dead in a year with nothing really to look forward to. Oscar Howe, the friend who placed said shithole play in my hand, was to read the rewrite today. I'd only skimmed it two hours ago. After meeting McNicky, I'd slept for fourteen hours. My dog was on strike, as I'd forgotten to feed her upon arrival home. She could barely look at me that morning.

I headed to Oscar's office, down the uncomfortably silent alleyway that housed a row of lawyers. Hoping none of them were Hammonds and Creek, I hurried along. I knocked once and headed in, all smiles. I placed it gently on his desk and waited for my magic to touch him.

The look on Oscar's face was similar to the expression of you having to piss for the last half hour but if you leave in the middle of someone's boring story you'll seem like an ass. Finally, eyes up.

"I see you've taken some liberties here."

Shit, I've offended. Well. He literally gave me olives and expected lemonade.

"Well, I've actually been thinking a lot about the dynamic. I mean, a woman singing in the woods, in this day and age. Leave her the fuck alone, right? She's doing okay without some bloke bothering her."

I guffawed. Silence. I begged the earth to swallow me.

"Thank God, you saw that too? I've tried to understand it and I simply couldn't." Oscar leaned back in relief. "I really like what you've done here, Lucas. Now we've got some serious investors from Spain coming in, making some moves in town throwing money at small theatres. Big fish theory."

"How the hell'd you swing that?"

"This writer isn't much of a playwright but he's a schmoozer. Young girls in Ibiza with rich daddies seem to love him and support anything he's up to, such as this play."

"But," and I'm incredibly careful with this, "I've completely rewritten it."

"I'm prepared for that. How is, 'written by Lucas Duncan based on the short story "Songbird" by Connor Jeffries?'"

"Fantastic."

"Are you still considering the role, you know, since you've taken liberties?"

He kept saying that. Decide if you want to make me feel bad or if you're grateful, old man, Christ. "Of course, Oscar. If you'll have me."

"Never gave anyone else a second thought. Are you ready to wow them again?"

"Absolutely."

Wowing was great, but money was also nice. I wasn't pushing the compensation conversation. Work is work, and residuals were drying up. And God did I need work. I suppose this was my cue to pucker up to Nancy.

I stared out the window of Nancy's office. Splendid view of Oscar Wilde's statue. I didn't dare turn around. Nancy was quiet, for lack of a better term. The quiet of sheer self-control to not to overturn anything in your path.

"I'll have you know that Jimmi is no longer with us."

"He's dead?"

"Quit."

Misjudged that one. Also I had to ask, "Is he suing?"

"He's been well compensated." Nancy's brow took on a quick furrow then disappeared.

That compensation must have stung like a sucker punch. I had to imagine that there was one: a particularly good reason he wasn't suing, or two: this new percentage was going to make my eyeballs bleed.

I was correct on both counts, as Nancy coldly continued.

"Jimmi had a little skimming issue. I had handed over a few newer clients which Jimmi hiked to nine percent. I'd have thrown a bottle myself. And as for you, I'm not pressing charges because I've heard you're pounding the boards again. And thank God for that."

Nancy can be supportive, yes, but genteel? Not likely. "Thank you, Nancy. I'm looking forward to it."

"Well, good, because I was having trouble getting your wizard and snake stories in front of eyes." She shuffled papers on her desk, not looking up for what seemed like ages. I wasn't sure if she expected a ring kiss or an exit. I decided to exit.

"Oh, Lucas, one more thing."

And here it is.

"I'll be adding that nine percent to this play. Meeting with Oscar was my idea."

I nodded, exited, and thanked God she hadn't had me hauled out of there. I needed a drink, and I hadn't spoken to Den since McNicky.

I walked into Den's dream bar to cheers and clinks of glasses. *Well, hell, this is dandy and nice.* And then I realized, it wasn't for me. It was for Den. Amongst were Den's Dad and Mum and maybe one brother whose face is so bland I constantly forget his name. Can't even fudge because the starting letter doesn't even come to mind. But it wasn't Den's birthday, that's November.

I scanned for decorations of any sort and saw a pink papier mâché maraca. I was lost. Den took a quick scenery sweep of the room. He landed upon me, his face dropped a little and then quickly corrected to a smile. I wasn't quite welcome. He headed over, sidling between his parents to reach the door.

"Hey, Lucas. How've you been?"

"Um, good, good. Just came from Nancy's, you wouldn't believe—"

"Uh Lucas, I'm sorry, we're having a little family gathering, my brother must not have locked back up when he stepped out for a smoke."

Wow. Den looked more on edge than I've seen him in his charmed life as of late.

"Oh sure, sure, so sorry. Parent's birthday?"

Den looked around to a stern-looking Rebecca. "Ah no, Rebecca is expecting, so were uh, just uh, you know bringing the family round."

Expecting. Interesting. Not interesting bad, just hmm. I've known every small thing that has ever excited Den. Every bit of good news he had, he couldn't even wait 'til the second tick to tell me.

Expecting, though. That was big news. And now I felt shafted.

"No worries, Den." I turned to leave, hand on the knob, "Just remember to lock back up."

One step outside, and of course it started to rain. How poetic. I then realized it wasn't a maraca, it was a fucking rattle.

I ducked under a canopy to light a quick smoke. The first drag was always the best. Of course, I was ruminating. Why didn't he share? How was it that I felt like I was interrupting the life of someone I've known since '84? A slight twinge of nausea caught my stomach. Lord, Lucas. It didn't matter. A rush of nausea passed over me and I headed towards the trains. Crowded and anger-inducing or not, I needed to get home fast. I wasn't at all feeling so well.

I hadn't talked to Den in weeks. No reach out. Radio silence. I hadn't even been round the pub as of late, so it might've been a "you, first" kind of thing. It was for the best though. I was dead to the world. Couldn't stand. Vomiting at water, gagging at smells. My Moleskine laid empty for days, couldn't even muster a tirade.

Memo 5

Let's call this *Patches*.

Bigger and better things were up since I'd shaken that horrible stomach flu. We were off book for the play. Correction, *I* was off book, and was setting out for my third interview of the week.

First up was Carol Feinstein with *Playwright's Hour*. God, I hated this woman, Rob Brydon in a wig. She's egregiously touchy-feely and comes off as if she'd just now done the research on you. But press is press.

We wrapped the fourteen-minute interview and exchanged pleasantries which were kind enough until—

"How are you holding up after the divorce, Lucas? That was quite a fervent affair."

My body almost collapsed in on itself and my stomach turned forcibly. Diana and I had been divorced for almost three years but the fallout, or rather, her constant gossip-rag grab for the spotlight made it seem that much more present.

"Quite fine, Carol, thank you." It was all I could muster. A small "hmm" escaped her, and she and her assistant turned on their heels and went. The assistant took another up-down peruse of me before a headshake of pity saw him out the stage doors. A slight flutter in my belly made me gag.

I was hoping I'd shaken this malaise and gut punch, but alas. I will tell you something quite strange. I was center stage that week, words pouring out of me faster than my mouth could carry, with nuance and meter and all the good dynamics one wishes for. I looked out at Oscar and his two assistants, their mouths agape, one on the verge of tears and I thought, I've sacked it. I was babbling like an idiot, surely. But no. They leapt to their feet at the close of the scene. It was exhilarating. Oscar had shaken my hand so hard my shoulder locked, but I could've run a mile. The melancholy of sick was snatched from me, I was grinning and couldn't stop. They say the outpouring of gratitude for your job well done releases post-coital amounts of oxytocin—a euphoria so to speak.

I'd done it. *Dammit, McNicky, you're a god.* The praise. It was back. I was back, in full force. A silver, no, gold lining to the miserable decade I'd been treading water in. But that's not the strange part. Oxytocin is fine, very fine. Until the pendulum swings so hard to the left that you're searching online for how to tie a noose.

Rounding the corner of Café Nero, I'd caught sight of another rag Diana loved getting attention from, *Click*, and firmly planted on the cover, was Diana and Oscar Howe in full lip-lock in front of some waterfall. I snatched it and slapped at the pages until I'd found the cover story.

"Do you know who's currently shaking the sheets with West End producer Oscar Howe? Actress Diana Pacheaux nee Duncan! Rumor has it that Diana's ex-husband, Lucas Duncan, also-ran extraordinaire, was barely scraping by to meet the alimony requirements, but has landed a big role in hotshot new play, *Songbird* that's offering him a big payday to which she earns fourteen percent. I guess everybody wins!"

And that's why Oscar was producing it, for her to cash in. I dropped the magazine and pounded the pavement, possessed.

My mouth was dry. The bile in my throat rose and I ran my hands through my hair. And the first pump of the pendulum: a large gather of hair rolled between my fingers.

And it all came up, everything consumed on the last day, I wiped my mouth hurriedly. Vomiting on the streets in broad daylight, a scar is born.

I'd completely lost myself somewhere between Café Nero and four blocks away. The wind was howling fiercely, and I caught a glimpse of myself in a store window. Einstein, fresh in the morning. And then I stopped, cold blooded. Sheer patches and white slips of flesh streaked my wild head. The wind had taken most of my hair along with it. I dropped to my knees and was clumsily caught by two women behind me. I popped up swiftly as I noticed a remarkably familiar profile. The second pump of the pendulum: Maria.

"My God, are you okay, sir!" Her voice rang throughout my entire body and every single follicle engaged.

Outline. Engage.

Everyone was looking, or no one cared, I couldn't decide which. And then I heard it, faintly but clearly.

"Christ! Lucas? Lucas!"

I sprinted home in pure agony, confusion, and shame. My most recent poisonous trifecta. I fumbled with the keys, because of course

I bloody would. I burst through the door and took one spin around the room and fell cleanly out. The dog would eat late again tonight.

My pants pocket buzzed with a vibration I should've enjoyed, but it only spun my stomach. I leaned on my side to fish out my phone. I felt the side of my face and it was hot to the touch, my forehead, blistering. I tongued the inside of my cheek. That iron taste of blood again. Had I mentioned I was vomiting that as well? I let it buzz.

I headed to the bathroom to take stock of myself, and I almost buckled. I was grey in some areas, red-and-black bruised in others. My hair was a virtual road map of black thickets and sand traps. My kingdom to see McNicky again. I hoped he'd pop up in the apartment like some grinning genie in the space between the edge of the couch and the silverware drawer in this studio flat. He was right, I couldn't take it.

"You mean to tell me people stopped liking you and you said OKAY?"

Yes, McNicky, yes. Two things were for certain in those days after meeting him. I'd feel overwhelmingly fantastic, or I'd vomit and wish for death. And then I realized, as I drew circles around the divots in my head on my reflection in the mirror, that McNicky hadn't given me my every desire, he'd cursed me with it.

My career was back on track, but that meant back in the spotlight and unfortunately, due to Diana's big mouth and even bigger wallet to finance a story, back in the gossip columns. Negative press. My body shuddered so hard, I needed to grip the sink to stay standing.

Maria was profoundly—and albeit disjointedly—back in range. I hadn't seen or heard from her in a year, since my email that could've been a rejection call.

I could wave off the naysayers and tabloid lies. I could act my ass off and get ahold of my career again. I could reach out to Maria. It could all be right. Right with the world and met at the middle, producing the fucker that sends me sky-high. But it felt wrong, and the pendulum sways got stronger.

I couldn't bear a bad word said. I knew I fucked up everything I touched, I didn't need someone telling me so. I knew I gave up too early and shut out opportunities because they were beneath me, I just didn't want someone telling me so. I knew I took all my fears and stresses out on someone I truly grew to love because running is easier than trying to resolve things. I couldn't—wouldn't get out of the loop. So, wrong it would stay.

I could manage wrong. Right takes more concentration, more time.

I laid on the couch with the dog and let the world fall away.

It was dark when I awoke. A green haze of light took over the kitchenette and the dog shifted and plopped down to the floor. I stumbled to the bathroom and refused to look at myself. I felt somewhat refreshed, in any consolation. Refreshed is excessive. It felt like that last full day of the flu.

I thought back to Maria on the street and broke into a cold sweat. She recognized me as this rotting shell—and a clumsy one at that—and I couldn't take it. I began to sob. She had come in like a whirlwind and, to completely save you from all the cliches, was everything I never knew I needed or wanted. She was younger but not by much, incredibly lovely, and graceful to look at, hilarious, driven, and passionate and most likely *the* most caring woman on the face of the earth. And I took her for the longest ride I could.

Non-committal one moment, only to plan a big trip the next. I pulled away and then showered her with compliments, the old push-and-pull that rode me through acting school. I was thinner then and a hell of a lot more charming. Jerking someone around was fun in your twenties but unbelievably stupid in your forties. I was stunted in that juvenile dickery of a man about town.

Diana and I were divorced for about a year and a half when I met Maria in a bookstore. I was blocking the aisle accidentally, and she brushed against me. Acting school lotharios are a dime a dozen, and I've had my share of zeroing in on someone I'd like to get to know better, but this, this was a thunderbolt right between the eyes.

"Oh, excuse me," she said timidly.

"Yes, oh God, I'm sorry." My mouth must have been agape because she looked at me and smiled warmly, then scurried around the corner. I followed as if carried by something—and I know this sounds so ridiculous and saccharine, but I could honestly tell you, I believed I had fallen in love at first sight. For the very first time, with anyone.

Her hair was a wild curl and it swung about her shoulders as she bounced from display to display.

I did my usual chat-up, and she called me on the sheer corniness of it. We laughed and had coffee that afternoon. The next day we had dinner. She went to Brussels for a month, and I literally thought I'd die. When she returned home, I told her I'd love for her to be mine and she happily agreed. A glorious year filled with passion and care and learning these new feelings of mine were love. Something I don't think I'd ever really had. Not with anyone. And on proper inspection, not with Diana. Just two bodies at their sexual peak and not much else.

I couldn't believe Maria was real. Or that *we* were real. How was she so kind, so concerned about me and my well-being and my hopes and future? It was alien. And I began to treat it as such. As word spread that Diana and I were clean cut-through with no further legal entanglements, a few friends I'd made over the years in the acting pool had cropped up. Friends of the "if only I weren't married" kind, and some took a keen interest in my whereabouts, my situations, and my commitments. And that's when Maria's ride went into full swing. And you don't have to tell me that I'm an absolute bastard and heathen who self-sabotaged a good relationship for the hopes of scoring a lay with a few fawned-after women. I know. I just don't want to hear you say it.

And with the gift of gaining something new, that meant something old had to break.

Maria tried everything she could to salvage our relationship. And I chided her with the well-this-is-just-how-I-am's and the I-guess-I-can't-do-anything-right's. And I'd pushed her too far. And so, I made the decree of just never speaking again. Never seeing her again. Ever. Cold turkey. And she gave up. And it had been silent for over a year.

And I was heartbroken. Because I'd made the rules.

A few times a week, I pillaged my laptop through hidden folders to find a slew of things I really should've stopped looking at.

Maria_Brussels1.mp4

Maria_Copenhagen.mp4

Maria_Me.mp4

On and on and on. I loved watching the light in her eyes when she was showing me around places she loved. Her smile in the videos of us about the house, her laughing at me being square and too studious. Some were naughty with a bit of flesh. Sometimes I talked to her.

And it was on that day I decided to drag my swollen body over to the desk and sit there for hours with Maria. And when those ran out, I switched to her voicemails.

Memo 6

Let's call this *Smudge*.

I'd ignored the haze of light in my kitchen for over three hours. I could only imagine there was a laundry list of texts from Diana, Nancy, Oscar. I was finished and would like to be left to my slow and agonizing death. The dog grunted near the door, and I owed this dog a hell of a lot more leeway than I'd given her. I tapped my phone screen. Six messages from Den. One from Rebecca. This couldn't have been good.

The pup and I struggled down the stairwell to the back-alley door of our flat. The air was heavy and foreboding like the minute before a thunderclap. I let the leash slacken and she headed to her usual wall and did the biz quite quickly, but spooked at a thick fog rolling in. I felt the remaining hair on my head bristle and inhaled so sharply, I heaved a heavy cough. I'd forgotten a hat to cover the mess of desert patches. I ran my hands over it in disgust and was so alarmed by what I felt that I instinctively yanked on her leash in panic.

My head was …

Full.

No desert divots. No fuzzy thickets protruding out of a sand trap. All there. Like it never left. I vomited a bit and wiped my mouth. Christ on a raft, I couldn't keep doing that. My dog was turning circles in the alley in distress. My hands were on my knees covered in streaks of blood. I begged God to just kill me.

A boom of a voice sent me spinning and I rocketed towards the wall, pulling my frightened pup toward me.

"Jesus. The hell happened to you?"

Christ on a cracker. McNicky. I was ablaze with anger, over what I'm not sure. All I know is that I'd have given anything for the strength to knock his fucking lights out.

"If you haven't noticed, I'm a little out of sorts here."

"Oh Lucas, I've noticed."

Fuck he's smug. "How did you know where I lived?"

"Who the fuck you think got you the Uber? You were swayin' outside the bar like a damned flag."

Right. It had been almost two months to the day of my fateful meeting with the Marvelous McNicky and I was either circling the drain of a nervous breakdown, or the specter itself has risen again. I blinked quickly as if it would all disappear. The alleyway, the thick air, McNicky. Nothing. I was knackered.

"Usually when I give someone something they want to live life to the fullest, they take the bull by the nuts and go skyrocketing upward. You, Lucas, have squandered a very, very precious opportunity."

"You've given me nothing but psychotic thoughts and a nervous stomach." I couldn't believe he was acting like a slighted fairy godmother. I was posted against the wall of the alley like a stapled flyer, and I couldn't seem to get my body free enough to approach him.

"I gave you an opportunity for praise. Praise. Praise, my good man! Praise be to God, if you're into that, and praise be to you. But you're too much of a sonofabitch to notice that the train came and went. You told me what you wanted, and I gave it to you and all you do is sit and whine, piss, and moan and for what? You couldn't even take it and run with it. You had to woe is me all over it." He cringed, making a crude ejaculation mime. "All over it!"

McNicky pinned me against the wall, manic. His eyes were wild and milky, and his mouth was larger and longer that it ever should have been. I started to scream, and his slimy and hot hand ran across my lips and slammed down with such a force, my jaw was on the verge of unhinging. The pup whimpered, and I was thrust down to my knees in the alley.

"I'm going to give you one last chance to take it all. Take it all and run. You want them to love ya and never stop loving ya, you better straighten up and fly right, you pissant, or it'll all go away as quickly as it came."

His breath was a mix of firewood and something rotten. I pulled my hand up to swipe at the lapel of his trench coat when I fixed upon a small protrusion near his scalp. Had he fallen? Mouthed off to the wrong Londoner? It wasn't until I gazed to the left and found a similar bump that I made the connection of McNicky's sore lack of humanity. His swollen lips drooled a thick white liquid as he panted in my face. I swiped at his face enough to push him off. I wiped maniacally at my lips. The taste of his hot sweaty hand was burned on my tongue.

"What do you want me to do?" I couldn't face him. I could only glance at his long, languid shadow on the pavement.

"Just have a little grace. A little appreciation for the gifts you're given is all. Outline. Engage. Embody." I felt him start to move on. I watched his shadow shrink, counted his footsteps in paces and measured mine to the back door.

"And Lucas?"

I couldn't help it. My eyes darted his way. Not a scratch or strand of slicked back pompadour out of sorts. The streetlight hit his forehead like a halo. Void of any terrain.

"I hope we don't have to meet again."

He began to whistle, and lightly stepped around the corner. His whistle was clear, throaty, as if played directly into my ear. The opening score to *Lifeline*, before Florence's stupid belly rub gesture sent my life tits up.

I couldn't tell you how long I'd been in the alley. Minutes. Maybe an hour or two. All I knew is that when I stood, I had more energy than I had in years. I practically bounded up the steps, the dog excitedly behind me. I walked slowly into my apartment as it was well past midnight and flipped through the messages from Den.

Where are you?

Are you alright?

Lucas, fucks sake someone told me they saw you and you looked terrible.

If something's going on, please let me know!

Lucas!

God dammit, Lucas!

And the one from Rebecca seemed to echo not as loving of a sentiment.

If you're not dead like my husband seems to think you are, answer his calls or I'll slit your throat myself.

That gem of a woman.

I messaged Den.

So sorry, I've not been feeling great these last few weeks, horrific bug. On the mend. Care to pop over?

At exactly 2:42 a.m., a soft rap on my door startled me. If it was McNicky, I swore to myself I'd slit my own throat. In that moment I was torn between answering the door and wrapping my brain around whether I'd made a deal with the devil. It'd been a nonchalance until just now and my blood was pulsing fast.

Another rap.

I flung open the door. Den lumbered in and pulled me so hard into him I lifted a little. I pulled away and slapped my shirt and slacks in a pout. He always made me feel like a toddler when he did that.

"You cunt." Den playfully shoved me.

"I'm sorry. It's been an incredibly rough few weeks."

"Too rough for a pint?" Den brandished a growler at me.

"Never."

"Aye, good." Den headed into my kitchenette. He knew his way around. Helped me find the place.

"So, what's the damage?" Den handed me a cool pint and settled into my other chair. A full couch couldn't dream of fitting its fat ass in this flat.

"Well for starters, I broke my agent's assistant's nose, almost lost my agent, got incredibly ill, found out Diana is screwing Oscar Howe."

"Ugh, gross. Why?" Den takes a hearty sip of his ale.

"Not sure. Threw up in the street, started losing my hair and, oh yeah, I unceremoniously bumped into Maria while looking all the more like the crypt keeper. I think that's it."

Den sat incredulously. And sipped slowly before responding. I hated it when he did that.

"Fuck. What got you ill?"

"Jury's still out. I think I've made some really bad choices lately."

"I'll say."

Den fished in his back pocket.

"I figured you'd want this back." He handed me my Moleskine book. My eyes welled. I hadn't known I'd lost it. All this time I'd forgotten how attached I was to that book, its exercise in atrocity and anxiety. My palms itched just to touch it. Maybe that was the sickness, no outlet to scream into, no place to put all my vitriol onto about this sick, sordid world, my haven.

"God! Where'd you find it?"

"Found it lying in the alleyway behind your flat when Rebecca and I swung by a week ago. Hadn't had a chance to give it to you 'cause you stopped coming by all together. Thought something was wrong so I've been trying to get ahold of you. There's some pretty sick shit in there. Disjointed and sad. But sick. Things really bother you that much?"

I was on the verge of passionately defending myself against a world determined to shit on me, but I paced myself. I hadn't seen the man in sixty days, my best friend of over thirty years, I'd let him off the hook for now.

"They're just random thoughts of the day. Minor annoyances are all. It's either that or going to jail for screaming my fool head off at someone."

"At any rate, I think you ought to talk to someone."

"Thank you, Diana."

"Oh, come on, Lucas. I'm just looking out for you. I'm worried, we're worried."

"Your wife threatened to slit my throat this evening."

"Just her way. Look I know it's none of my business, but you doin' okay? Money-wise?"

My eyes rolled clean to the back of my head and Den quickly shifted direction.

"I just mean, I know the play is on next week and that'll be a sturdy sum."

The play. Fuck. Was I losing time?

I must've had a disturbed look in my eye because in a flash Den was kneeling by my chair with his hand on my shoulder.

"Hey, you alright?" Den squeezed my shoulder and twisted to set his glass on the counter.

"Yes, yes, just hoping the immune system continues to hold out." I smiled weakly and Den seemed satisfied. He headed back to his chair, and it was nice to have my friend back round again and of course I ruined it because my mind was partially on McNicky and all his fuckery and the play and Maria and the fact that—

"Why wasn't I invited to Rebecca's baby shower?"

Den's face fell and he clasped his hands in prayer and settled his forehead upon them. He sighed deeply.

"Because we were being incredibly careful about celebrating. She's in the substantial risk bracket. We've lost two now, so we wanted to keep it close for a while."

"I see."

"She's got to stay off her feet from here on out so I'm training a few new guys on the ins and outs at the bar. She's happy for the rest, but we worry."

There's a bend in his eyebrow I don't think I'd ever seen before. It sunk into me. Absolute pain. Part of me wanted to rush to him and give him free rein to cry. Part of me was stunned. I never thought of Den wanting children. I'd only thought of him and Rebecca as this united front forever and ever amen. Children for them seemed maddening. Den was the most patient man alive and Rebecca, well Rebecca was abrasive. Reminded me of my mother. And with that I shuddered so hard it shook words out of me so fast my hands couldn't catch them to put them back in my brain where they belonged.

"Let's hope she does a better job of holding onto this one."

Den glared at me but said nothing.

Damn. Now I'd done it. I stood as Den made his way past me. I grabbed his arm, and he shrugged me off. He stood with his back to me for what seemed like a lifetime. I loved Den more than my own brother and I don't know why I'd said that. In the back of my mind, I'd had an inkling. Daddy Den wouldn't have the time to manage my drivel and deprecation, point blank, and it would be easier to divorce Rebecca if it came down to it, without any children. It crushed me. McNicky was right. I really am a sonofabitch.

"Keep the growler. We've got more than we can stock at the bar anyway. Good to see you're well, Lucas." Den headed to the door and my feet cemented to the floor. My eyes welled and while my mouth hung open, nothing came. And nothing that would come would have been worth Den wasting his time for.

"Oh." Den turned and I was full of promise again. My feet dislodged and stepped forward. As I did, Den took a step backward, putting absolute distance between us. "I also saw Maria, came in with a few friends for a hen do. Not hers, a friend's. She asked about you."

"What for?" The surprise took my voice up an octave.

"I guess because she's concerned. She's the one who told me you weren't well."

"Anyway, I gave her my ticket for the play. She'll be coming round."

I felt my whole head cave in as I grimaced. "Are you serious?" I couldn't tell if I was angry or elated. The thought of seeing Maria in the flesh was enough to make my head spin and I felt a dizzy spell coming on. I gritted my teeth to hold it together.

"Hope you two can patch things up. God knows she deserves better. Break a leg, Lucas."

"Den?"

Den shut my door quietly and I heard him gently pad away in his usual long stride. And I stood there in the low lamplight of my kitchenette watching the door, half expecting my only friend to pop back in with a jab and joke. But I got nothing, and I knew I'd just lost the absolute best person. So, I emptied the growler for the next hour and headed to my computer.

It was time to practice my chat-up with Maria.

Memo 7

Let's call this one *Quandary*.

It'd been ten days without incident and by incident I mean no projectile vomiting, no missing hair, no extreme fatigue, and no coughing blood. I felt completely energized, almost on high alert. And I've lost so much weight with the previous illness that I finally look fit in my clothes, but on proper inspection I was almost concave, and wardrobe was pissed. Oscar was curt but enjoying where we were in performances. Industry night was a smash and I'd done at least five interviews a day since, both print and video, and I was determined to make McNicky proud.

I'd told no one of him or my hell-bound handshake with the menace, but I felt that I'd been given a new lease on life, and I was determined to not only put things on the profitably straight and narrow, but to get my woman back. I searched for her in every audience. Maybe she'd come already and now we wait, or maybe she'd be here tonight. The daily eagerness and sizzle of it sent me and every night I tried to knock it out of the park for her and her alone.

There was a new fella in the stage crew that particular night. He seemed very astute and took an incredible amount of notes. Jack, his name was, I guess. That's what wardrobe called him with a lilt in their voice. They hushed about him when I came round. It was odd.

I headed to Oscar's side room to settle the who's who of the audience that I should be spotting and plotting to, and I stepped out a bit as I noticed he was on the phone. Then the hush made sense. I'd be finishing out my week and would go on the last night of the run. They were giving new man Jack my role. Turns out he was an all-out sensation as Mercutio in *Romeo and Juliet* and Orlando in *As You Like It*. He was bucking for the new run of *Sweeney Todd*, I heard the dresser say. My fists were so tight my middle fingernail had worn into my palm. I rapped anxiously on Oscar's door, causing him to frantically spin and arrest the call.

"Lucas! Come in, my boy! Full house tonight."

"Yes, I was just finding out who our press target is tonight."

"Oh, I wouldn't worry about that, just head out there and give me what you've been giving me for the last weeks. It's been damn fine."

Don't do it Lucas, don't fucking do it. Don't say a fucking word.

My lips burned with anger, but my smile kept my mouth from opening. The hall was electric. It was as if everyone had a static attached, we were all smiles at each other and wide-eyed. It felt good. All the while there was a pit deep in my stomach called *my farewell tour* and I felt more on the spot than usual. Not dry, mind you, just swinging for the rafters on this one.

For most of the play, the theatre is pitch dark, just outlines of bodies and figures but at the line, "But be the grace of all that's wild and free," all the lights kick up in sparks, exhibiting my love for the mysterious woman of the wood.

I turned to the spotlight and spoke the words. The edge of the stage erupted in a million sparkling lights and silk overlays, and it was in that light that I caught it. The silhouette of wild curly hair. I turned ever so slightly to catch the brown eyes I've longed for, for the last year. Her eyes danced in amazement at the lights, silks, and music as I had watched them dance at every international monument she lovingly explained to me on her travels. It was everything I'd been waiting for, and I did what I'd dreaded doing ever since *Lifeline*. I went off the book. And I spoke so deftly about love and its trappings and its hang-ups. About the mark true love leaves on you and even when you shut it out or turn it away it stains your soul like a bloody ink drop and if you're lucky enough to glance upon it in your lifetime you'd better grab hold with both hands and not let go. And I directed "Not. Let. Go." to a hand clasped Maria whose eyes had welled.

A shun of silence, and that pit in my stomach grew but turned towards the sunlight of a thunderous applause. For three uninterrupted minutes I stood in position, and gestured longing at the back of a no-doubt agitated head of Kiara, our lead, still waiting for her reveal. As a crew, we clasped hands one last time together. I hugged just about everyone, Kiara twice because she was just so proud and thankful. I headed to wardrobe, changed into my sweats, and washed off my rouge.

One last knock at Oscar's office. The door was ajar, so I let myself in and ran headlong into a morbid-looking Jack.

"Everything alright?" I said, maybe a bit too musically.

Oscar grimaced and patted Jack on the back. "No, everything is not alright. Lucas, that was indeed an absolutely splendid performance. But we've got a problem here."

"Oh?" *Lucas, you cad.* "How so?" I said.

"Jack here was to be going on for you for a bit of the run. And now we've got to figure out what the hell you said tonight."

"Yes. I heard. Earlier."

"So, you've heard the news?" Jack jumped up, elated. "So incredibly exciting!"

Lucas, don't.

But I couldn't help it because of course I bloody would. "Exciting?" I turned my bulging gaze to Oscar. "Oscar, you hire some young dandy hack to replace me, without so much of a word. Who's bringing them in every night, lining your pockets while you're sleeping with my ex-wife?"

Oscar's eyes widened, embarrassed. I didn't back down.

"Me! And to think you're going to toss me out on the street for it? Got your pansy to make a quick buck for her? Well fuck you, Oscar, I'm out!" The blur hit me something awful and I rushed past everyone in a shot. I made it out to the street and finally took an inhale. And sobbed. Man alive, I sobbed like a child.

There are so many times in our lives that things ring familiar. A scent from long ago leaves you cuddling within it, and it places you back. But other times it's a sound, guttural and ancient, and it throws you back to a time where you would have done anything to escape it or anything to stay within its presence. A gob-smacking sound hit my heart and mind all at once and I spun so hard I nearly fell over.

"Lucas?"

Maria stood at the edge of the back alley of the theatre, her coat pulled close to her.

"They said you'd come this way. You were wonderful tonight." She stepped forward and I froze. Feet, lips, everything. I must have looked disgusted. She backed away quickly and headed left.

"Well, I, uh, I just wanted to say excellent job."

A heavy figure loomed behind her with two other men in tow. Oscar, some sheepish, thin man holding an umbrella over Oscar's head when it wasn't even raining, and some jar-headed barnacle.

Oscar stood toe to toe with me. "Just when I thought you couldn't sink any lower, Lucas, here you stand, at the bottom of the barrel. Never has anyone talked their way out of a career-defining role quite like you. I'm sure Diana will be pleased to know she doesn't have to hand out favors to you anymore."

"Career-defining!" Through tear-stained eyes, I, a grown man, was shouting, but I knew it this time. "You were ready to throw me out on the street for it! For what? So some younger, hotter, playbill playboy can take the role? Make his career defined?" I was air-quoting. I hated it when people did that.

I cowered a bit as Oscar moved closer. He was taller than I remembered, perhaps because I was scared or perhaps because the woman I wanted most in the world was watching it crumble.

"Lucas, I asked Jack to fill in because I wanted you to have a chance at booking *Sweeney Todd* on the West End. They already liked you and thought you'd be a sure winner, but formalities are what formalities are. I figure you could use the time off to run lines and prepare. I also added a go-see to your calendar with Nancy about the lead in two book adaptations. You've got the right stuff, Lucas. Improvisation is something special and you brought down the house tonight. But I'm afraid I'm going to relieve you indefinitely and I'll no longer be referring you or taking your calls."

"Oscar." I reached out my hand and he took one look at it and stepped back.

"Not only do you jump to conclusions, but you're also quite ill at understanding. Evening, Lucas, and the absolute best of luck to you."

The men drove off in a black town car that pulled up on cue. I couldn't tell if my body was going numb from shock, shame, or if the old ticker was finally doing me in. I felt a hand on my shoulder, and I jumped. Maria looked somberly at me.

"Oh Lucas, I'm so sorry."

The time was 11:40 p.m. GMT and I was standing outside what felt like my very last job in theatre, in anything, for as long as I lived, which at the rate things were going, shouldn't be awfully long. And a woman I couldn't tell I loved her until we stopped speaking completely was standing by my side and hoping for the best for my future as she always had. Again, here we were. Me, downtrodden and self-loathing, her, a beacon of hope and love. And I couldn't be more grateful—or angrier.

Front row, she sat. Front row. I could only think *Den wouldn't even chip in for mezzanine without a fight from Rebecca.* She had to have purposefully tried to throw me off. And I went off, into the most overly sentimental bullshit-laden soliloquy since *Love's Labor's Lost.* I've dreamt of her, practiced things I'd say at this very moment, and I was dry.

"Why are you here?" My voice was gruffer than I meant to be. Her eyes narrowed. *Oh Maria, what's happening?*

"I—I just wanted to see you, I'm happy you're back doing theatre, you always loved—"

"Oh, Christ's sake, after all this time, you're curious? Supportive? You sat in the front to throw me off, didn't you? Well, it worked, are you happy? Happy I'm out of a job because of your antics!"

"Lucas, I always sat in the front row. That's what support means!"

"Well to hell with you, I made the best decision, so please, go!"

Maria backed up and walked steadily backwards. Her eyes were dead, her face, a road map of curious lines and lips that trembled. Those lips. Those lips painted on the same canvas as those God damned eyes that skipped my heart even while my blood pulsed in angry spurts in her presence.

Oh, Maria, my love. These words aren't mine. Lucas. The fuck are you doing?

Maria turned on her heels and walked quickly up the street. And I watched as she grew smaller and smaller and finally turned the corner, out of my life forever.

A weak and slow applause caught me by surprise, and I dared not turn around because the smell of cinders took over my lungs.

"I swear if I had a dollar for every numb nut that couldn't follow directions, this coat would be mink." McNicky walked out of the alleyway just a touch. "I was hoping we wouldn't be meeting like this again, but, since you like things the hard way, here we are."

"Just kill me already, McNicky. The hell are you waiting for?" Everything I ever thought meant anything was gone. Maria, Den, my career, my wherewithal, all dust.

"Easy Lucas. Bylaw's state I've gotta tell you why I'm here."

"I don't give a fuck about your bylaws, McNicky."

Something sharp, hot, and stinging took me out at the ankles, and I was face down on the pavement sliding frantically backwards. It slithered me over to McNicky, now perched in the alleyway, hairs bristling, forehead protrusions glistening in the faded streetlight that crept into the darkness. His lips were swollen again and his hands still hot and wet but now adorned with claws the length of my face and eyes full of fire and white-hot heat. I felt myself screaming, and he inhaled the sound so quickly, it got lost in the dark as if nothing happened at all.He whispered his putrid breath in my ear. I jostled, ankles still bound by what seemed like his tail.

"Now," he panted. "The reason I'm here is because you simply can't help but keep looking a gift horse in the mouth. You see, I've been hearing about town that you're on about one hundred people's shit lists and they'd give anything for you to trip and fall on the sharpest object on the planet and put yourself out of your own misery. So of course, being thorough at my job, I gotta find you and check you out. No way so many people hate one sonofabitch so bad, right?"

I squirmed again and he tightened his grip on my chest and my ankles.

"So, I find you, meet you, and see, hey, the guy ain't so bad, a little bit of a whiner but hey, life ain't always a beach, you get me? But then we start talking, and I get the feeling you just drain the whole goddamn world with your poor me act, why me, me, me, me, me! Christ almighty, day in day out, the world just fucking hates Lucas Duncan on sight, right?"

"Yes!" I managed to whimper out.

"No! You just can't take the sun getting up and shinin' before you had a chance to. You're one of the worst people in the world, you know that? Selfish, arrogant, narcissistic pricks that think a minor inconvenience is the same as someone coming up and stabbing them for no fucking reason. Get a life!"

He let me down gently.

"I gave you a shot, the energy to make a hit play. What do you do? Complain? Give you a chance to see your friend's world don't revolve around you and try to have you find other things to occupy your time than bitchin' his ear off but no, gotta take it personal, I give you a chance to have the love of your life back. You blame the bitch for inspiring you, for fuck's sake. What's wrong with you? Never in all my centuries of living have I ever met such a waste of life as you! I ain't gonna kill you, Lucas, you're already dead! You been dead! A dead man walking for the last thirty years! And now I'm gonna take it all away, all the chances, all the grace."

He let my ankles free.

"It's too bad you live on praise and attention. When you don't get it I see you ain't been feelin' so good. So, you better get runnin' home, now, Lucas, before you toss your cookies again!" He laughed maniacally and it echoed through my entire body. I desperately wanted my feet to move. "Run!"

He charged me and my feet engaged.

"Run, Lucas, while you still got a body that'll move! So long you stupid shit! Good luck!"

His laugh reverberated through the buildings and street, it shook the streetlamps and set off car alarms. I rushed home so hard, my lungs were on fire. I wiped the sweat from my brow and streaked a tuft of hair with it. My eyes filled with tears, and I had to jerk myself out of the path of cars and buses. I wanted to end it all, I wanted it all to go away.

Oh, McNicky. You bastard. Just fucking kill me.

I nearly broke the key opening my door and find an RSPCA notice that my dog "should be given to those who care to give it it's best chance." My home was a dull orange from the kitchenette light, and Noomi lay silently on the floor. She didn't greet me anymore. On the counter, a note from my landlord gleamed white against the ginger haze.

Sorry, Lucas, we've had some complaints about excessive barking during the day. I'm not sure if you've gotten new work hours or you just haven't been home, but pets need care. The pitiful thing looks a little emaciated. The RSPCA is offering to house her until she's fattened up a bit or until you're settled, and she can get the attention she deserves, or you can waive your rights to her so they can put her up for adoption. Again, really sorry.

—Ted

It was just as well. Poor Noomi, she deserved better. They all did. Maria. Den. Diana. Oscar. Nancy. They've had their lives imbrued by the stain that was Lucas Duncan.

Good riddance to a dead man walking. I vomited again and fell clean over in a heap.

Memo 8

Let's call this one *Epilogue*.

I'd had a nice woman from the RSPCA take Noomi, poor love needed a live human to care for her. Not a shell. She licked me on the nose and took off with the woman, staring lovingly at her. It's the last charitable thing I'll accomplish.

I woke today to a bright beam of sunlight hitting my face. For a moment all felt right, it was quiet. I grabbed the cleanser and baking soda from the cabinet and began to dress the new vomit stain on the carpet. I'd become a pro at this. It's been three days since I'd unceremoniously left *Songbird*, since Maria made the best choice possible and since McNicky helped a hundred angry souls finally eradicate one Lucas Duncan.

I made my way to the bathroom and shouted at the look of myself. My eyes were all but blackened underneath and bloodshot. My fingernails were turning a sick green hue. My hair, well there was none, and I appeared to have lost at least two stone overnight. I've also sweated through my clothes. I stood over the toilet for a leak, but nothing comes. I rinsed my mouth out with water and spat out two teeth in the process. I could've sobbed but I understood. I knew the rules and I broke them. Could've just gone with the flow, could've been happy with the new riches in my life or recognized promise as it came. But no, not my style. I'll die by my own hand as well.

So, I'm sure it'll make sense why I've set up the computer, chopping this ridiculous story into bite-sized bits because one bloke droning on for hours is no one's cup of tea. I just wanted you to know why I did it all. The notebook, throwing the glass at Jimmi, bleeding Den's energy dry, battling Diana, dreaming of Maria, wanting fans instead of friends and lovers. I simply could not get out of my own way.

And McNicky is a thorough bastard. Praise *was* keeping me alive, and love. Love was too, and whether it was healthy love or past memories, my heart was hopeful. I don't believe in that anymore. Because you see, Maria was saving my life. The hours of footage were a lifeline of sorts, but in anger and fear I deleted all her videos. What a mess I've made.

Of everyone and everything I've touched. Here lies Lucas Duncan, Shit Midas.

It won't be long now, and I apologize for all the time you've spent.

I've been living off Maria's voicemails and just yesterday a car alarm terrified me right in the middle of a message causing my cheek to delete all messages. She's gone. Gone forever in space and time. Never knowing my earnest heart. Me never sharing it. Maybe you'll tell her.

I always kept all the good lines to myself and unleashed all the vitriol and bellyaching upon the world.

So, if you ever come upon a nice fella from Queens, NY with a great head of hair and a devil-may-care attitude, I'd act like the happiest, shit-together chap you know and be aware and aloof. He found you, so there's a bounty on your head from someone, somewhere. Straighten up, bucko, and fly right. You get one George Bailey a lifetime, so don't blow it. I think that's everything. And if anyone that's out there that's ever cared a lick about me could grant me one final request, for my headstone, I'd like it to read:

Lucas Duncan
Born October 8th, 1970 – Died August 11th, 2017
You can't be fucking serious.

Goodbye.

About the Author

Mo Moshaty is a genre screenwriter, author, and lecturer. With a concentration on psychological and possession horror in her writing, Mo's background as a Trauma Specialist and Behavioral Therapist provides a sturdy foundation. She is the creator of the course, "Writing Trauma Respectfully for Screen" and was a Guest Lecturer for Prairie View A&M University's Film and TV Program and with Horror BAFSS in Sheffield, UK for No Return: A Yellowjackets Symposium.

Mo is a journalist, and co-founder with Nyx Horror Collective and co-producer of the 13 Minutes of Horror Film Festival featured on The Shudder Channel. Nyx Horror Collective was founded by a group of diverse woman-identifying horror creators to develop, celebrate, and elevate original, women-led horror content.

As a core member of Nyx, she has recently partnered with Stowe Story Labs to provide a fellowship for women writers over 40 working in the genre. Mo also served as Associate Producer on Scottish Indie SciFi Horror web series, "Cops and Monsters", and was ecstatic to shine more of a light on indie horror. Mo's most recent literary work can be found in *A Quaint and Curious Volume of Gothic Tales*, published by Brigid's Gate Press and "206 Word Stories" by Bag O' Bones Press.

Twitter: @MoMoshaty
Website: www.momoshaty.com

Acknowledgements

Though we may never travel to the depths of these lost souls, take this time to lean into your mirror, and acknowledge the hellish thoughts within all of us. For we all carry a Greg, a Jacob, a Collin, an Agnes, a William, a Benjamin, an Eli and a Lucas.

Bless you all. I hope you make it.

Content Warnings

Death or dying
Excessive graphic and/or gratuitous violence
Mental illness
Suicide and/or self-inflicted harm

MORE FROM BRIGIDS GATE PRESS

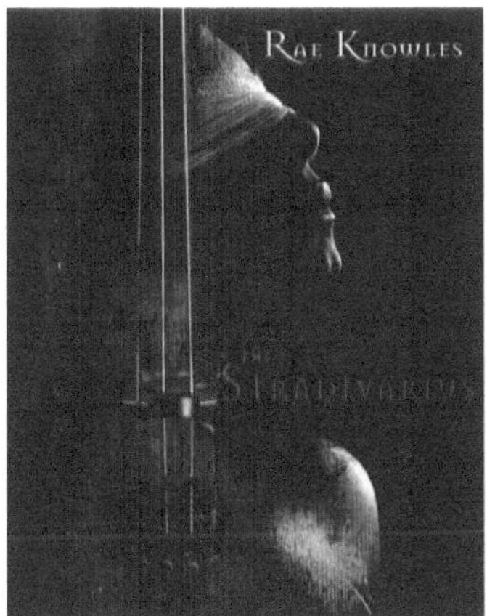

When a surprise inheritance and whirlwind romance offer Mae a chance to escape her repressive aunt, she's all too eager to elope and start life anew in her childhood home. But when she and her new husband arrive, the towering Victorian sits in disrepair, and Mae learns that her father's decade-old, unsolved murder is still a source of rumor and speculation in town.

Leading the charge to unravel the mystery surrounding her father's death is Ollie, a vibrant genderqueer and an outsider in their hometown. Sure that solving the cold case will land them a coveted job in the police department, Ollie gains access to the Victorian by agreeing to do maintenance work on the property.

Inside, Mae is taunted by a feminine specter, soft voices from empty rooms, and distinct melodies of Lady Paola: the priceless, Stradivarius violin stolen the night of her father's murder.

Forte, mezzo-forte, the measured, andante cadence.

Her hiss, her pull, her scream.

Mae fears the house is haunted by her father's spirit, her husband believes she's going the way of her mother–slipping into madness, but Ollie suspects something more sinister is at play. If Ollie and Mae can't work together to uncover the Victorian's secrets, Mae will join her mother in an institution or her father in the grave.

The settlement of Grey's Bluffs is a prosperous town. An independent community dwelling in the shadows of the mountains known only as The Hungers.

Esther Foxman and Siobhan O'Clery have grown up in Grey's Bluffs, thriving out on the western territories in the aftermath of the Civil War. Devoted to one another and their home, the two set out to complete a regular pact at the Hungers to ensure that Grey's Bluffs continues to prosper.

Cyril Redstone is a man who knows death well. Becoming a mercenary after the Civil War, Cyril leads the marauding Blackhawks from one slaughter to the next. Hired to destroy Grey's Bluffs, Cyril cares little for morality, nor that he owes its founder his life.

Esther and Siobhan are left to defend the only home they have ever known from the Blackhawks, their confrontation driving them deep into the mountains.

Where the darkest secrets of the Hungers await them.

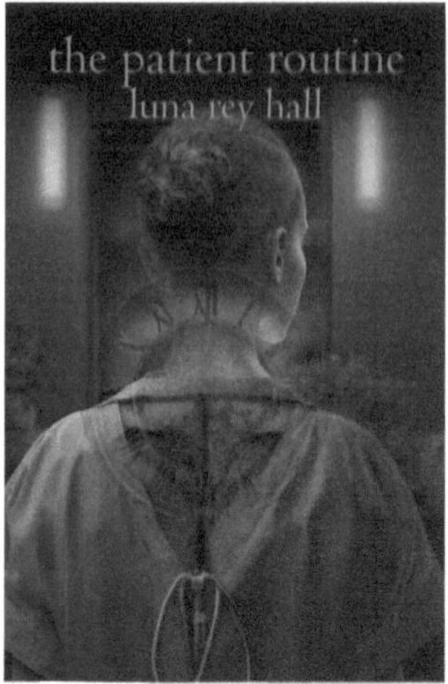

Ashton is convinced they are dying. whether it be from cancer, heart disease, or a fungal infection, they know something bad is always about to happen. after a night of health-related panic attacks, & urged by a voice in their head, Ashton decides to check in to the ER again but when another patient is brought in with an unknown ailment that puts the entire hospital on lockdown, Ashton may be trapped in their worst nightmare.

Following the death of a loved one, Rachelle Collins visits Ferguson Estate, an expansive country mansion which holds many fond memories, and one sinister secret, within its walls. Throughout the course of a single, terrifying night, Rachelle must confront horrors, both psychological and tangible, to prove just how far she is willing to go to keep her family together.

Visit our website at: www.brigidsgatepress.com

www.ingramcontent.com/pod-product-compliance
Lightning Source LLC
Chambersburg PA
CBHW031246210726
48287CB00003B/911